Henceforward . . .

A Play

Alan Ayckbourn

Samuel French – London
New York – Sydney – Toronto – Hollywood

ISBN 0 573 01691 7

Please see page v for further copyright information.

HENCEFORWARD . . .

First presented at the Stephen Joseph Theatre in the Round, Scarborough, on 30th July, 1987, with the following cast:

Jerome	Barry McCarthy
Lupus	Robin Herford
Zoë	Serena Evans
Geain, aged nine	Victoria Horsfield
Geain, aged thirteen	Emma Chambers
Corinna	Penny Bunton
Mervyn	Michael Roberts

It was subsequently presented by Michael Codron at the Vaudeville Theatre, London, on 21st November, 1988, with the following cast:

Jerome	Ian McKellen
Lupus	Robin Herford
Zoë	Serena Evans
Geain, aged nine	Victoria Horsfield
Geain, aged thirteen	Emma Chambers
Corinna	Jane Asher
Mervyn	Michael Simkins

Directed by Alan Ayckbourn
Designed by Roger Glossop

CHARACTERS

Jerome, a composer
Corinna, his wife
Geain, their daughter
Zoë, an actress
Mervyn, a welfare officer
Nan 300F
Lupus ⎫
Young Geain ⎭ (seen on video only)

Nan 300F is played by the same actress as Corinna in Act I and by the same actress as Zoë in Act II.

The action takes place in Jerome's studio in North London

ACT I   SCENE 1   Friday night/Saturday morning
         SCENE 2   A few hours later

ACT II   A week later

Time—sometime quite soon

Other plays by Alan Ayckbourn
published by Samuel French:

Absent Friends
Absurd Person Singular
Bedroom Farce
A Chorus of Disapproval
Confusions
How the Other Half Loves
Intimate Exchanges (Volume I)
Intimate Exchanges (Volume II)
Joking Apart
Just Between Ourselves
Living Together
Mixed Doubles (with other authors)
The Norman Conquests (complete volume)
Relatively Speaking
Round and Round the Garden
Season's Greetings
Sisterly Feelings
A Small Family Business
Suburban Strains (musical)
Table Manners
Taking Steps
Ten Times Table
Time and Time Again
Tons of Money (revised)
Way Upstream
Woman in Mind

One-act play for children:

Ernie's Incredible Illucinations

ACT I

Scene 1

Jerome's studio. Friday night/Saturday morning. Sometime in the future

The living-room of a flat. It's a curious room. No windows, or, at least, what there were are curtained off and no light comes through the heavy steel shutters outside. There is a sofa, two swivel chairs and a low coffee-type table—all modern. That's really the extent of the recognizable furniture. The remainder of the room is filled with some very sophisticated electronic equipment. Not an amateur electronic rat's nest of wire and cable but custom-built units containing computers, tape and disc recorders—racks of amplifiers, filters, reverb units and gismos of all descriptions. At one end, several keyboards. Some of these are covered and remain so until much later in the play when we realize for the first time what a vast array of equipment Jerome actually owns. The room, in fact, betrays the contradictions in his own character. For while the immaculate technical equipment is kept lovingly protected from the slightest speck of dust, the rest of the room—the living area—is in fair chaos. Remnants of instant meals, old tea and coffee cups, the odd item of clothing. The signs of someone who lives alone and has stopped caring much. And, strangely, the overall impression given off, despite all the modern paraphernalia, is of something faintly Gothic. Three ways off, one to the hall and front door, one to the kitchen and one to the rest of the flat—the bedrooms, bathroom, etc.

When the Curtain *rises, the room is dark. The only light is from a video/sound console system, at present inactive. We can make out very little or guess the time of day. All at once, a large wall-mounted video screen lights up. Or perhaps a series of screens. We see the picture as from a front-door video entryphone system*

Jerome, a man of about forty, can be seen at the door. He is carrying three carrier bags, together with a somewhat incongruous walking stick. We see Jerome inserting his key and struggling and muttering as he opens his front door. He enters the flat. As he closes the front door the screen blanks again. After a second, the hall Lights come on and Jerome approaches down the hall. Then the Lights come on in the living area

Jerome is standing in the hall doorway having just switched on the lights. He dumps his packages on the sofa and replaces his stick near the hall doorway. Also on the sofa, slumped, face down in a somewhat undignified posture is Nan, who remains motionless for some time. Jerome, ignoring her, crosses to the console, where he switches on his answering machine. As he moves back to the sofa, on the screen and through the speakers, the machine fast-rewinds. He doesn't take much notice of it, though. He gathers up two of the carriers which appear to be filled with tinfoil-sealed instant meals and starts to go into the kitchen. As he does so, the answering machine starts to play back both sound and vision. An introductory beep. A logo appears: The Department of Social Services. ECONOMY. Except in special circumstances all calls made are NVR. 01-993-9000

Mervyn's voice Mr Watkins, this is Mervyn Bickerdyke from the Department of Child Wellbeing . . .

Jerome groans

I've been trying to get hold of you for some days now, regarding a meeting. The time is nine forty-six. I wonder if you would call me. My number is on screen. Thank you.

He hangs up. The screen blanks, the audio beeps. In a second, the next message appears

Jerome (*on his way to the kitchen, in reply to Mervyn*) No, I won't and I'm not.

Jerome goes into the kitchen

A fanfare-like tune from the answering machine and a logo appears: BLAISE GILLESPIE—Escorts for the Discerning

Choir (*singing, from the video*) Blaise Gillespie! A call from Blaise Gillespie!
Voice (*cheerfully*) Hallo, Mr Watkins, this is Mary Hope-Fitch, calling once again from the Blaise Gillespie Agency. It's ten-forty on Friday. Just to remind you of your appointment today with Zoë Mill who plans to be with you by fourteen hundred this afternoon. I hope that's still convenient. She's looking forward so much to meeting you. We feel certain she'll answer all your rather specialized requirements. If there's any problem at all, please don't hesitate to call. Thank you.

Jerome returns from the kitchen for his third carrier bag

Choir (*singing, from the video*) Blaise Gillespie! A call from Blaise Gillespie . . .
Jerome (*mimicking them*) From tone-deaf Blaise Gillespie . . .

Another couple of beeps as the message ends and moves on to the next. It is the same logo as the first call

Mervyn's voice Mr Watkins, this is Mervyn Bickerdyke, Department of Child Wellbeing . . .

Jerome groans. And goes into the kitchen with the carrier

It is urgent that I speak to you. I realize you may be—busy with your compositions—but it is a matter of some importance. It's eleven seventeen and my number is on screen. Thank you.

Jerome returns with one of the tinfoil food packages in one hand, a palm-sized section of printed circuitry in the other

A beep as the message ends on the answering machine

Jerome Look what I've brought for you. (*He balances the circuitry casually on Nan's back as he passes her*) Who's a spoilt girl, then?

Jerome sits on the sofa and studies his purchase. Another beep. The screen crackles and flickers with a fuzzy image that could be anyone's

Zoë's voice (*faintly*) Hello, this is Zoë Mill. I'm from the Blaise Gillespie Agency. And it's eleven fifteen . . . Hallo? Hallo, this is Zoë . . . Hallo? Can you hear me? Oh, dammit . . .

Another beep. The screen clears. Jerome, unperturbed, continues to read. Another beep. Interference as before, if not worse

Hallo, this is . . . Oh, Jesus! Don't any of these bloody things work at . . .?

Another beep as Zoë is cut off. Jerome reads on. As he does so, there is a swift beep—a yell from Zoë and another beep—qualifying as the shortest message ever

(*In fury*) Aaarrrgggh!

From the machine, another beep and Lupus appears on the screen. He is a forlorn sight, a harassed, careworn man in his forties. He wears a T-shirt reading MUSIC IS A *LIVING* THING. *It appears he is at home, from the background we can see behind him. The sound of a child playing out of sight*

Lupus's voice Hallo, Jerry. It's me. Lupus. I thought I'd just call you, mate . . .

Jerome, reacting to Lupus's voice, gives a terrible groan

. . . keep you up to date with how things are——

A ball, presumably thrown by a child, bounces off Lupus's head. The child laughs

(*Ineffectually*) Ah, now don't do that, Orson . . . That hurt Daddy. The point is, Jerry, it's come to the big N.C.H. Ultimatums from Deborah. Threats from the Bank Manager. I mean real threats, Jerry. Two heavy lads in camel-hair coats kicking at my front door. So it looks like I'm going to have to take that job with those geriatrics. I never thought it would get this desperate, Jerry. Look at me, I'm a top session-player——

He is struck again by a projectile

Orson—don't do that, darling, Daddy's talking—Jesus—what am I reduced to—?—relief drummer in a three-piece band for an old folks' dance in Finchley. Who needs it, Jerry? Answer. I need it. Desperately I need it.

Jerome, apparently following the instructions he has been studying, removes the tinfoil package from its sleeve and searches for an insulated surface. In the end he decides to place the container on one of his discarded items of clothing, a shirt, which he spreads on the coffee table

My God, I do. Because there's nothing else. But I don't have to tell you.

Jerome, having positioned his container, holds it in one hand, and tugs at a red ring in the lid. This pulls out a length of metal strip which he is left holding in his other hand. He stares at both items suspiciously. Jerome, during the next, goes to the answering machine, tossing aside the packet sleeve

And if Deborah leaves me, Jerry, which it looks as if she's going to—it's sorting out the suitcases time, you know—but if Deborah goes—on top of everything else ... I mean, I've been a loving husband. I've been a forgiving husband. God, have I been forgiving? I let her play around with—every bastard who could make it up our stairs. Present company excepted. I just don't know what I'm going to do, old mate ...

Jerome pushes a button on the console and Lupus goes fast-forward mode. He spools jerkily on for some time. The child-aimed missile hits him on the head as his high-speed twitters on. Jerome finishes his instructions. He shrugs and moves over to Nan, picks up the printed circuit card and examines it. He goes to a cupboard beneath the console and gets out a large loose-leaf manual. He studies this. As he does so, Lupus's message on the tape ends, the machine beeps and resumes normal speed. Another beep. The screen reads: FAULT: VISION TEMPORARILY INOPERATIVE

Zoë's voice (*rather distraught*) Hallo. This is Zoë Mill from the Blaise Gillespie Agency at—God, what's the time?—it's twelve thirty-one—All right? I've been trying to phone you for ages—Only none of the—And I keep getting your machine. My train is—my *bloody* train—pardon the language—is delayed—and I'm now at—God knows where I am—Oh, where the hell am I? Just hold on a second.

Station sounds as, apparently, she opens the call-box door

(*Calling to someone*) Excuse me! I say, excuse me. Could you tell me where I am, please? ... Where? ... Hendon Central? Thanks so much.

The door closes

Hallo, I'm at a place called Hendon Central, apparently. So I don't know when I'll reach you. More important, I hope you're there because I'd hate to think I—— (*She is interrupted by a series of beeps*) Oh, I've no more on my card, that's it. See you shortly. I hope. Otherwise I——

The screen goes dead and then reads: MESSAGES END. *Jerome remains impervious to this. He is still intently studying the manual. After a second, the screen blanks*

Jerome (*at length*) All right. Let's see what we can do. (*He rather unceremoniously puts his hand up the back of Nan's skirt and fumbles for a moment*) Pardon me. (*There is a click and his hand re-emerges with an identical piece of printed circuitry*) Ah-ha!

He studies it critically for a moment and then throws it aside. His hand goes back under her dress as he replaces the circuit with the new piece. There is a series of clicks

(*As he does so*) Now . . . I'm not supposed to be doing this, you know . . . If they caught me doing this . . . they'd . . . aaah! . . . get in . . . they'd probably lock me up and melt you down for scrap . . . I had to steal this from a check-out machine at the supermarket when their backs were . . . aah!

A final click

Nan (*a little sigh*) Aaah!
Jerome Ah! There you go. Good girl. Now.

He heaves Nan round and sits her up on the sofa

God, you're a heavy old bag of bits. Come on.

He grabs her neck on either side, brings it sharply forward and then back. Nan clicks. A male's voice, decidedly not hers, probably a long forgotten technician's, emanates from somewhere in Nan

Voice NAN 300F, series four, model 99148622G for Gertie. System check commencing—Go.

Nan goes through her pre-check routine. This is rapid and comprehensive. A great deal of internal computer chatter as systems load. Her eyes blink rapidly, her mouth flaps, every joint of her body tenses then relaxes. She rises, sits, her limbs jerk

Nan (*in her own voice, very rapidly*) Modified Sampling Commences. Oh-for-God's-sake-Jerome-can't-you-think-of-anyone-else-but-yourself-for-a-change-just-for-once-I-mean-what-sort-of-a-person-are-you? Modified Sampling Ends.

A few more whirrs and clicks

System check complete. Operational eighty-three point one seven. We are sixteen point eight three per cent unstable and are within eight point one seven per cent of permanent shutdown. (*Cheerfully*) Clock set o-eight-hundred hours. Good-morning. Rise and shine.
Jerome Nan, walk about.
Nan Walk about, Nan.

She does so. She walks with a rather bouncy stride but has a slight limp. She clanks a little as she goes down on her bad leg. Jerome watches her critically as she circles a couple of times

Jerome That's better. You're not bumping into things like you were. I've still got to fix your leg, though. It's the pivot. You need a new pivot, old girl. Only they've stopped making them, you see.
Nan (*banging into a piece of furniture*) Oh, for goodness' sake, you extremely stupid old bat. Who put that there, then?

This last reveals the slightly tetchier side of Nan. In fact, as time goes on, we see that she is rather a Jekyll-and-Hyde creature. Her sunnier nature is the result of her initial "nanny" factory programming; her darker side the result of subsequent modifications by Jerome himself—the source of which will become clearer later

Jerome Nan, come here.
Nan Coming, Nan.

Nan comes to him and stops in front of him

Jerome That's it.

Jerome crouches down and lifts her skirt to examine her knee. We see that at the knee joint her legs cease to be humanoid and are exposed metalwork. Nan licks her fingers and starts to smooth Jerome's hair

Nan That's better . . .
Jerome Don't do that . . .
Nan That's better.
Jerome Nan, stop.
Nan Stop, Nan.

Nan stops. He rises

Jerome Nan, watch my finger.
Nan Watching your finger, Nan.

He moves his finger to and fro in front of her eyes. She follows it with her eyes very slowly

Jerome Yes, I think we can sharpen your reflexes a bit.

He places his hand inside Nan's blouse while continuing to move his other hand in front of her eyes. Nan's response quickens noticeably

That's it . . . that's better . . .

Nan suddenly twitches violently

Whoops! Too much. Sorry. That's it. Nan, thank you.
Nan Thank you. Lovely glass of orange? Lovely orange?
Jerome Nan, lovely.
Nan Lovely. Lovely morning. Rise and shine.

She bounces off to the kitchen

Jerome (*glancing at his watch*) Oh, I never set your clock, did I? Never mind. You're better than you were.

He goes to the console and plays with a few switches. From the kitchen a crash

Nan (*off*) Oh, for goodness' sake, you extremely stupid old bat. Who put that there, then?

Jerome frowns but ignores the sound. He puts on some Bach. It relaxes him. The phone rings. He makes no effort to answer it. It continues to ring

Jerome Go away, Lupus, I'm not here. (*He notices suddenly that his meal is still sitting there in its tinfoil*) Oh, no! (*He grabs hold of the tinfoil package.*

It is very hot. Dropping it) Ah! *(He picks it up with the shirt it was standing on and cautiously, still protecting his hands, he opens the lid. The contents are black and charred and smoking. Disgustedly)* Oh, miraculous. *(He drops the tinfoil back on the table)*

Nan comes in with a mug in her hand. It is unfortunately empty since she is holding it upside down

Nan *(placing the inverted mug on the table by Jerome)* Lovely glass of orange. *(Heading towards the bedrooms)* Lovely morning, wakey-wakey.

Nan goes into the bedroom

Jerome *(staring at the mug in disgust)* You load of old scrap. *(He is about to drop the shirt, too, when he observes that it now has a burn mark on it, left from the heated tinfoil. Equally)* Oh, mind-numbing. *(He lies on the sofa for a moment absorbing the music)*

Nan enters with a face flannel in her hand. She makes a beeline for Jerome

Nan *(playfully)* Booo! Nan's coming to getcher!

Nan attacks his face vigorously with a flannel. Jerome struggles. She is apparently quite strong

Jerome Waah! Noff.
Nan Come along, wash your face and hands before your breakfast!
Jerome Wah! Noff! *(Getting his mouth clear)* Nan off! Nan off!

Nan stops at once

Nan That's better.
Jerome I am reprogramming you. You've taken a layer of skin off my face. You do that again and I'm stripping you down for spares and then dropping you off a twenty-storey building——
Nan Story-time, now ...
Jerome Oh, God ...
Nan Once upon a time there were three bears called Jack and Jill who wanted to go to the ball only the other ducklings wouldn't let her play with them ...
Jerome Nan, stop.
Nan Stopped, Nan.
Jerome Nan, register.
Nan Register, Nan.
Jerome *(standing in front of her so she can scan his face)* Not child. Not child.
Nan Not child. Registered, Nan.
Jerome Nan, take a nap.
Nan Take a nap, Nan.
Jerome *(muttering)* I don't know why I bothered to switch you on again, really.

She heads back to the bedrooms

Nan (*turning suddenly tearful, in her other tone*) I don't know why I bother, Jerome, I really don't. When you treat me like this. I've done everything I possibly can. I can't cope any more. If you want to go and live with her, I don't care. Go on! Go on! Go and live with the bloody woman. See if I care.

She goes out to the bedrooms

Jerome frowns. He sits. The Bach continues to play. After a moment, there is a crash from the bedroom. Jerome gets up

(*Off*) Oh, for goodness' sake, you extremely stupid old bat. Who put that there, then?

Jerome sits once again and closes his eyes, assured of peace at last. After a second, the doorbell rings. The screen lights up once more. It is the video entry-phone system again. Zoë is at the front door. She is breathless and dishevelled

Zoë (*from the screen*) Mr Watkins ...
Jerome (*disturbed again*) I don't believe this ...
Zoë Mr Watkins! This is Zoë Mill from the Blaise Gillespie Agency. Would you let me in, please? (*She looks anxiously over her shoulder and rings the doorbell again*)

Jerome crosses to the console. He switches off the music

(*Urgently*) Mr Watkins! Please!
Jerome (*pressing the door button at the console*) All right! Push the door.
Zoë Mr Watkins, open the door ...
Jerome Push it. It's open ...
Zoë Oh, please say you're in. Please God you're at home ... (*She rings the bell again*)
Jerome (*yelling*) It's open. Push the door!
Zoë I'm going to break it down, Mr Watkins.

We see her, on screen, step back and run at the door. Jerome presses the door button long and hard. Zoë hits the door which opens easily. She disappears

A second later, she appears in the room, a tattered, breathless wreck. She pulls up short, breathing heavily

Jerome stares at her incredulously

(*Attempting a semblance of dignity*) Mr Watkins? How do you do. I am sorry to burst in like this. My name is Zoë Mill. From the Blaise Gillespie Agency.

Jerome stares at her stupefied

(*After a pause*) I hope they advised you I was coming, I ... (*She trails away*)

On screen, the view of the hallway remains

Jerome (*suddenly aware of this*) You've left my front door open ...

He rushes out of the room into the hall, seizing his walking stick as he goes

Zoë, alarmed, flinches slightly as he dashes past her. Jerome appears briefly on the video screen. We see that his stick is in fact a swordstick which he has now drawn. He checks to left and right, then closes the door. The screen goes blank

Jerome returns, sword still drawn

Zoë watches him, transfixed. Jerome sheathes his sword and replaces the stick near the door

Never leave my front door open.
Zoë (*muted*) No. I'm sorry. (*Pause*) You see, there were these people——
Jerome I know there are these people. Why the hell do you think I keep it shut?
Zoë Yes.

Another pause. Jerome stares at her. Zoë tries to pull herself together. It is difficult for her. Her clothes are in ribbons, her face is bleeding from a cut and her hands are torn and filthy. She has lost one shoe and is holding the other. Her stockings are in shreds. She obviously started out looking quite elegant in her smart suit and crisp blouse

Jerome (*aware he has been rather rude*) Sorry.
Zoë No, no. I'm sorry. (*Brightly*) Well, here I am. At last. (*She laughs nervously*) What a super room.

Jerome is staring at her. A pause

(*Nervously indicating a seat*) Is this—for sitting on?
Jerome (*guardedly*) Yes.
Zoë Well. Would you mind if I ...?
Jerome No.
Zoë Thanks very much.

She sits. Jerome continues to stand, staring at her. She gives a sudden, quite unexpected, reflex sob as the shock begins to take hold but elects to continue as if it hadn't happened

I'm sorry if I'm looking a bit of a—I must do a bit. I'm sorry. Anyway, I understood this was just an initial interview. Mrs Hope-Fitch told me you just wanted to look at me. See if I was suitable. But I believe the actual job's not for a week or so? Have I got that right? (*She sobs*) Excuse me. Yes?
Jerome (*thoughtfully*) Yes.
Zoë (*indicating herself*) Look, you'll just have to disregard all this. I mean, *this* is ghastly. But I can—you may not believe this—I can look pretty good. Although I say it myself. Yes? But as I say, not—Don't, for God's sake, go by this. (*She sobs*) Sorry.

Silence

Would you like me to—walk up and down? Give you an overall picture? People sometimes find it helps them to—get a more general ... Of course,

I don't know quite what you're looking for so it's a bit . . . I understood it was slightly unusual? Is that so? (*She sobs*)

Jerome (*thoughtfully*) Yes.

Zoë I'll stand up. (*She does so*) There.

Jerome studies her

Five foot four and a bit. I can lose a bit more weight if you like. I'm a bit over my usual . . . (*She sobs*) I'll walk about for you. In case you need me to walk. (*She walks about, limping slightly*) By the way, I don't usually limp, of course. Please, disregard that. I just seemed to have bashed my knee—Anyway. And, naturally, with heels on I'm that bit taller. They help no end, of course, with all sorts of things. God, look at my legs. Don't look at those, either. I'm sorry, I'm afraid you're just going to have to take my word for an awful lot of things. (*She sobs*) Look, I'm awfully sorry, I think I'm just going to have to go away somewhere and have a quick cry. I'm sorry, I'm just in a bit of a state. I am sorry. Is there a . . .? Have you got a . . .?

Jerome Oh yes, yes, sure. There's one just out there. First on the left. (*He indicates towards the bedrooms*)

Zoë I'll be as quick as I can. I'm so sorry.

Zoë plunges out of the room. As she reaches the offstage bathroom door, we hear the sudden start of her tears, then the slamming of the door

Jerome stares after her, thoughtfully. He goes to his console and winds back a tape. He replays a section

Zoë's recorded voice . . . all sorts of things. God, look at my legs. Don't look at those, either. I'm sorry, I'm afrai——

Her voice cuts off as Jerome stops the tape. He shrugs. He switches the machine back to record. He waits. He fades up a fader on the panel. Zoë's sobs are heard over the speaker and the sound of her blowing her nose

Zoë (*over the speakers*) Oh, dear God . . .

Jerome fades her down and moves away from the console

After a moment, Zoë returns with a handful of tissues, wiping her nose

Sorry about that. Here I am. Back again. Anyway, where was I? Yes. Let me tell you about me. I'm originally an actress. Still am, actually. Only I also model to keep the wolf occasionally from the door. And I've been doing this escort thing lately which has been very interesting. Only I understood you didn't just want an escort, you wanted something slightly more. So that's probably why they thought of me. I did have some pictures and my CV to show you as well, only they took my briefcase. (*Getting tearful again*) It wasn't even as if there was anything in there . . . Sorry. There were these terrifying girls, you see . . .

Jerome Girls?

Zoë Who attacked me. Just now. On my way here.

Jerome Attacked you?

Zoë Girls. Women. I don't know.

Jerome What did you do to them?

Zoë (*rather indignantly*) I didn't do anything. I was just quietly walking here from the station. It was a lovely day and I——

Jerome *Walked?*

Zoë Yes.

Jerome You walked from the railway station to here?

Zoë Yes. I've just said. And then these monsters . . . came from nowhere. What sort of area is this? Don't you have any police at all? Any security patrols?

Jerome Not any more.

Zoë Neighbourhood vigilantes?

Jerome Not lately.

Zoë You mean, this area is not protected? At all? What about this building?

Jerome The security staff kept being found dead. It got very expensive . . .

Zoë My God. Mrs Hope-Fitch might have warned me.

Jerome What did these people look like?

Zoë Oh. (*She shudders*) Awful. No hair at all. Not on their heads, anyway. Masses of it everywhere else. And sort of purple paint across here. (*She indicates a band across the middle of her face*)

Jerome No, that's a tattoo.

Zoë Really?

Jerome They're the Daughters of Darkness.

Zoë Oh. They were female then.

Jerome Most of them.

Zoë Well, whatever they were. I didn't stop to introduce myself. I hit the biggest of them and ran as fast as I could . . .

Jerome (*stunned*) You hit a Daughter of Darkness?

Zoë Yes. On the head. With my shoe.

Jerome Ah.

Zoë Am I supposed to have done something wrong?

Jerome Well, I don't think you should have done that.

Zoë Why not?

Jerome Well, you may have got them angry.

Zoë Angry? What about my briefcase . . .

Jerome Was there anything important in your briefcase?

Zoë No, I've just said, just my——

Jerome Then it would have been simpler to have given it to them.

Zoë But I don't see why I should have just handed it over. It was a present from my ex-boyfriend.

Jerome You may have made things difficult.

Zoë (*sarcastically*) Well, oh dear, oh dear. That's all I can say.

Jerome For you.

Zoë How do you mean?

Jerome Well. When you want to get back, they may not let you back . . .

Zoë You mean . . .? But . . .? How do I . . .? I can't stay here indefinitely, can I?

Jerome No, no . . .

Zoë If they won't let me out, then we'd better call the police, hadn't we? Or whatever it is that passes for the law round here ...

Jerome I'm afraid that's them. They pass for the law round here. They are the law.

Zoë The Daughters of——

Jerome Darkness. Yes. Currently.

Zoë Well, in that case, I'm sorry. I had no idea I was hitting a policeman, I can assure you. Where I come from they don't have purple stripes tattooed across their faces. You mean this is a genuine no-go area? My God, I've only read about them till now. Mind you, I've never been this far up the Northern Line before. Where are we? Somewhere extraordinary. Edgware. I went to Balham once but that's the other way, isn't it? How absolutely terrifying. So what happens now?

Jerome It's all right. I'll talk to them. I have a relationship with them. Of sorts. I do things for them, now and then.

Zoë Do what?

Jerome I help rig their sound gear when they have their big concerts. Things like that.

Zoë Oh, how interesting. Are you a roadie?

Jerome Not really. It's just a hobby.

Zoë What is it you do?

Jerome I'm a composer.

Zoë How amazing. Well. Hence—(*she indicates the sound console*)—hence all that.

A sudden violent clang from one of the windows. Zoë is startled

What on earth is that?

Jerome That's the Daughters.

Zoë What are they doing?

Jerome Throwing bricks at the window shutters. They're showing their displeasure.

Another clang. Zoë winces

It's all right, they're half-inch steel. They'll probably keep this up for an hour or two. Till they think of something else to do.

Another clang

Zoë Lucky you had your shutters closed.

Jerome Hardly lucky. They're welded to the window frames. They haven't been opened in four years.

Another clang. She winces

Zoë They can't get in, can they?

Jerome Not unless they can jump thirty feet. It's all right.

Another clang. A silence

I think they've gone.

They listen again

Yes.

She relaxes slightly. A pause

It's quieter where you live, then?

Zoë Yes, we're—pretty lucky in Kilburn. Regular armed patrols, masses of security cameras and so on. Very well lit, most of it. I mean, actually, the High Street's brighter at night than it is in the daytime. Providing you're in by dusk you're fine. I've had no trouble. Not really. Couple of burglaries, that's all. Oh, and my dog was shot, that was sad, but we think that was an accident. We think someone must have mistaken him for a police dog.

Jerome Shame. We?

Zoë My ex-boyfriend.

Jerome Ah.

Zoë He's still living with me but he's definitely my ex-boyfriend. Still. Enough about me. To business.

Jerome Yes.

Zoë You must tell me about this job you'd like me to do. Assuming you'd like me to do it, of course?

Jerome Yes.

Zoë You're still deciding?

Jerome Yes.

Zoë Oh, right. Sorry. Do you want me to walk up and down again?

Jerome No.

Zoë (*laughing*) I could do you a bit of Shakespeare. Any good? No.

Jerome I wonder if you'd mind—trying on some clothes.

Zoë (*suspiciously*) What sort of clothes?

Jerome Just normal clothes. Women's clothing.

Zoë I'm the one trying them on?

Jerome Yes.

Zoë Where? I mean, where do you want me to try them on?

Jerome Here.

Zoë You mean in front of you?

Jerome Yes.

Zoë You want me to change my clothes in front of you, is that it?

Jerome No. I want you to change into different clothes elsewhere. And then come in here so I can look at you wearing those different clothes in front of me. That I'll give you. To wear. You.

Zoë (*considering this proposition*) Yes, that sounds OK. I'm sorry. It's just occasionally, you know, we get—sort of weird requests, you know. The old favourites, you know. Nuns and gymslips.

Jerome Oh, no.

Zoë Fine.

Jerome Nothing like that.

Zoë No, sorry. Just thought I'd . . .

Jerome These are my wife's clothes.

A silence

Zoë Your wife's?

Jerome Yes. They're quite ordinary clothes. They may be a bit out of fashion but——

Zoë Your wife, is she . . .?

Jerome What?

Zoë Is she dead at all?

Jerome Dead?

Zoë Yes.

Jerome No, she's——

Zoë She's still alive?

Jerome Yes.

Zoë Living with you?

Jerome No. We're separated.

Zoë Oh. (*She breathes more easily*) I'm sorry.

Jerome If you don't mind my saying so, you seem rather wary.

Zoë Well. Yes. I'm sorry. Look, this is my first time. As an escort. And I was assured that there was nothing further entailed, other than escorting. But then I get here and find you on your own, asking me to try on clothes. I got panicked. Sorry. I'm a little bit shaky still, I . . . Give me the clothes. I'll put them on for you. No more questions. (*Slapping her own face*) Zoë, grow up and be your age.

Jerome Wait there.

He goes out to the bedrooms

Zoë looks about her

Zoë (*to herself*) Nevertheless. This is a very, very creepy set-up. It has to be said.

She wanders about looking at the room for the first time, intrigued by the console. She is examining this when the doorbell rings and the nightmarish face of one of the Daughters of Darkness appears on the screen, leering into the video camera

Oh, dear God, it's them . . . (*She hurries towards the bedroom doorway*) Mr Watkins . . . Mr Watkins . . . I think it's them. They're at the door——

Jerome hurriedly returns with a long dress, similar to the one that Nan was wearing, a blouse and a pair of shoes

The face remains on the screen murmuring inaudible obscenities

(*Indicating the screen*) There! That's one of them.

Jerome Oh, she's OK. That's Rita. She's our local representative. She's fairly friendly. I'll have a word with her. (*Handing her the clothes*) Try these. The dress should be all right. I don't know about the shoes. We can always buy some others.

Zoë Don't let her in here.

Jerome Certainly not. She's not that friendly.

She takes the bundle

He picks up his swordstick and goes out

After a second he appears on the screen and we see him and the Daughter of Darkness engaged in an inaudible, urgent-looking conversation. Zoë, rather nervous now she's alone, glances at the screen, notes Jerome is busy and decides to change where she is. She undresses to her slip. There is a small sound from the direction of the bedrooms. Zoë starts, glances at the screen, hearing nothing more and seeing Jerome, relaxes again. She sits and, taking up the clean blouse, is fiddling with one of the fastenings on it, prior to putting it on

Nan appears in the bedroom doorway

Zoë does not see her. Nan watches her for a moment, then produces her face flannel

Nan (*playfully*) Booo! Nan's coming to getcher!

Zoë turns, sees her, but is too late to dodge. She screams. Nan sets about Zoë's face with her flannel. Zoë screams and struggles but her cries are mostly muffled. Unnoticed, Jerome finishes his on-screen conversation. In due course, he closes the front door on Rita and the screen blanks again

Zoë (*spluttering*) Hot hoo hooing hoo hee? Het ho! Hoff! Het Hoff!
Nan That's better. That's better. There's a nice clean face.

As she says this, Nan goes off at speed to the kitchen

Zoë (*calling after her, indignantly*) What were you doing? What did you think you were doing? Oh, dear God.

She grabs up the clothes and prepares to flee towards the front door

She all but runs into Jerome

There's a—There was a——
Jerome Anything wrong?
Zoë A woman just came in and washed my face——
Jerome Oh, yes.
Zoë What do you mean, "oh, yes"? Who is she? What was she doing?
Jerome It's all right, she registered you as a child, you see. That's all.

A crash from the kitchen

Unless she's told otherwise she registers everyone as children.
Zoë Who is she? Is that your wife?
Jerome No, no. She's a NAN 300F. She's a machine. She's just a machine.
Zoë *That*—was a machine? I don't believe it.
Jerome Oh, yes.
Zoë Well, what is it? Where did it come from?
Jerome It—er—it came from the man just down the hall, actually.
Zoë The man down the hall?
Jerome Yes.
Zoë I'm going. All right? I'll borrow these clothes. I promise to post them

back. I'm sorry, I don't think this job is for me after all. I think I'll just
stick around a little longer and hope for a fringe revival of *Hedda Gabler*.
(*She makes to go into the hall*)

Jerome Are you thinking of leaving?

Zoë I most certainly am. I'm not stopping here with that—deranged
machine, thank you very much.

Jerome I—wouldn't go just yet ...

Zoë Why?

Jerome Well, I don't think the Daughters would be too happy if you tried
to leave. Not until your case comes up before Council.

Zoë Council?

Jerome They're considering it at the next Council.

Zoë When's that?

Jerome Midnight.

Zoë Midnight? I'm not sitting here till midnight ... I mean, they can't ...
I've got masses of ... They can just—they can simply go and——

A single loud clang on the shutters

(*Facing the inevitable*) What happens at midnight, then?

Jerome They'll consider your case.

Zoë Do I have to be there?

Jerome Not unless you want to be.

Zoë No, thanks very much. What'll happen?

Jerome Rita thinks you'll get away with a fine. It would have been worse
but—I put in a word.

Zoë (*sarcastically*) Lucky I met you, really.

Jerome Do you have money with you?

Zoë I'm not a complete idiot ... I have credit cards on me.

Jerome (*curious*) Where?

Zoë Never you mind. Will they do?

Jerome Possibly. I know they take cheques. Listen, do you want to— (*He
indicates her state of undress*)

Zoë Oh, yes. Since I appear to be here for the night, I'd better get dressed, I
suppose.

Jerome There's a bedroom along there if you——

Zoë Where is the thing?

Jerome In the kitchen. It's all right, I'll keep her away.

Zoë Please do. (*She moves to the doorway*) There aren't any more of them,
are there?

Jerome No. Second door on the right.

Zoë Won't be long.

She goes off to the bedrooms

*Jerome frowns, as he is still undecided about her. He crosses to the console and
fades up a fader*

(*Through the speakers, muttering*) ... trapped in this place till midnight
with a raving lunatic and a homicidal tin woman is hardly my idea of a
good time ...

Jerome fades her down. He stops a tape machine and rewinds it a little. He replays a section. The voices come over the speakers

Zoë's recorded voice (*spluttering*) Hot hoo hooing hoo hee? Het ho! Hoff! Het Hoff!

Nan's recorded voice That's better. That's better. There's a nice clean face.

Zoë's recorded voice (*indignantly*) What were you doing? What did you think you were doing? Oh, dear God.

Jerome stops the tape and rewinds a fraction. He replays again

What were you doing? What do you think——

(*He rewinds*)

What were you doing?

Jerome (*stopping the tape*) No. (*He shakes his head*) No, no, no.

He hears Zoë returning. He hastily switches on the recorder again and moves away from the console

Zoë enters. She has on the dress, blouse and shoes

Zoë The clothes are fine. The shoes are a fraction large but . . . What do you think?

She poses to allow him to inspect her. Jerome studies her from several angles

Jerome Does your hair . . . Does it come down at all?

Zoë Oh, yes. Do you want me to . . .?

Jerome Would you mind?

Zoë No. (*She takes the clips from her hair*) I don't usually wear it down because it makes me look about ten. But—if that's what you're looking for . . . There! Is that more the thing?

Jerome (*impressed*) It's—it's excellent.

Zoë Oh. Good. Well. Good.

Jerome Excellent.

Zoë You still haven't really said . . .

Jerome Would you mind laughing for me?

Zoë Laughing?

Jerome Is that possible?

Zoë Yes. Hang on. That's one of the things I'm never very good at. I can cry very well. Floods of tears at the drop of a hat. No? OK. (*She tries*) Ha! Ha!

Jerome looks dubious

Sorry, that was awful. I can do miles better than that. Ha! Ha! No. Think of something funny, Zoë. Ha! Ha! You don't happen to know any jokes, do you? No, I didn't think you did. Ho! Ho! Ho! God, this is awful. Thank heavens my drama teacher isn't here. Haw! Haw! Haw! (*As her laughs get progressively worse*) Look, could we leave it for a second and come back to it. I could do you my piece of Shakespeare . . .

Jerome No, that's quite all right. Don't worry at all. I realize it must be very——

Zoë Well, it is very difficult if you haven't any real—motivation, you see.

Jerome Oh, yes.
Zoë I mean, frankly, not an awful lot's happened to me recently that makes
  me want to scream with laughter.
Jerome Please don't worry at all.
Zoë So, you want me to walk about with my hair down, laughing in a long
  dress . . . Any other requirements? I mean, what's it all for? Are we selling
  something?
Jerome Please. Sit down.
Zoë Thank you. (*She sits*)
Jerome Just a moment.

He moves to the console again, this time looking for a video recording from the
cupboards. Zoë waits patiently

  Nan enters from the kitchen. She carries a drinking glass and a plate, both
  of which are upside down

Zoë, frozen, watches Nan

Zoë (*in a whisper*) Mr Watkins . . . Mr Watkins . . .
Jerome (*from the cupboard*) Hallo?
Zoë It's—it's back again.
Nan (*putting the things down and turning to Zoë*) There we are, doesn't that
  look lovely? Doesn't that look good?
Zoë (*nervously*) Oh, yes. Lovely, lovely . . .

Nan moves swiftly to her, producing a coloured bow from her pocket which she
fastens in the protesting Zoë's hair

  (*As Nan does this*) Ah, now—don't you—don't you start that—Mr
  Watkins . . .
Nan There! There! There!
Jerome (*seeing what's happening*) Oh, yes. Sorry—it's all right, you're
  perfectly safe . . . Nan, stop.
Nan Stopped, Nan.

Nan freezes by Zoë, who escapes, looking slightly ludicrous with her hair now
in a top-knot

Jerome She's still registering you as a child, that's all. We'll re-register you,
  then she won't bother you.
Zoë Anything. I mean, I know my hair like this makes me look younger but
  this is ridiculous . . .
Jerome Could you just stand facing her, so she can scan you.

Zoë stands some distance away

Zoë Like this?
Jerome A bit closer. Would you mind?
Zoë (*moving closer*) I don't like the way it's looking at me.
Jerome That's just your imagination. She's not thinking of anything. She's
  actually on standby.
Zoë Yes, I think I've acted with one or two people like this.

Jerome Nan, register.
Nan Register, Nan.
Jerome Not child. Not child.
Nan Not child. Registered, Nan.
Jerome There we are.
Zoë (*stepping away*) Is that it?
Jerome Yes. She's now recorded you as an adult—well, rather as a non-child—so she shouldn't bother you at all now.
Zoë (*removing the hair bow gingerly*) Was it designed to look after children?
Jerome Yes. Well, technically, narrower than that. To look after a child. It was felt that the programming got too complex to deal with several children. So it was designed to deal with just one individual. Then that was it. It shut down automatically and you had to give it a whole new factory programme. It was a safety measure to prevent one being reused, you see. On a mismatched child. Well, so this man was telling me . . .
Zoë This would be the man down the hall.
Jerome That's right.
Zoë Why did he give it to you?
Jerome Ah, well. He was a designer for the firm that made them. But they went bankrupt and he moved away. He really only left me this for spares. I got her working again myself. Just for my own amusement, really.
Zoë But how can it still work? I mean, I thought you said they shut down once they . . .?
Jerome Yes, they do. I don't think this one's ever been matched to a child, though. She's a prototype.
Zoë You mean that's why she thought I was . . .
Jerome Yes. She lives in hope. Don't you, Nan?

Nan reactivates at the sound of her name

Nan I'll do the beds now. Time to do the beds.

Nan goes off towards the bedrooms

Jerome Random programming. If you don't tell her what to do, after a time she just selects something from her memory.
Zoë Seems quite sad, in a way. Wandering about, looking for a child to look after. Unfulfilled, almost. In so far as a machine can be unfulfilled, of course. I suppose no more so than, say, a coffee grinder that can't find any beans to grind could be described as unfulfilled.
Jerome Well, there's more to her than a coffee grinder. (*He sits*)
Zoë Oh, yes. But one mustn't empathize with machines, must one? They say that's fatal. Mind you, I do that all the time. I shout and scream at my washing machine. (*She laughs*) There! That was quite a good laugh, wasn't it? Why did they go bankrupt? The firm that made them? I'd have thought they'd have sold like hot cakes. What happened?
Jerome Er . . . They were very expensive. And—(*he seems evasive*)—there were teething problems.
Zoë (*suspiciously*) Were there?
Jerome (*reflectively*) I think the biggest mistake they made was to make a

machine so sophisticated and then give it too small a function. I mean, I think a machine that complex needed more than just a child to look after. Otherwise there's bound to be stress.

Zoë Possibly. Yes. What an interesting theory. You mean, a machine with a certain sized brain can actually have too little to do?

Jerome Too little to think about.

Zoë Yes. Quite a theory.

Jerome That's why I tried for a time to . . .'

Zoë To what?

Jerome Give her some other thoughts. Feed in other memories. Particularly with her having no child, I thought it might . . .

Zoë Did it help?

Jerome I don't know that it did, really. Still. It was worth a try.

A silence. He seems steeped in thought again. Zoë studies him

Zoë Did you say you were a composer?

Jerome Right.

Zoë What sort of music do you compose?

Jerome All sorts.

Zoë I mean, is it—you know—popular sort of music?

Jerome Not very, no.

Zoë No, you know what I mean—as opposed to classical music?

Jerome I don't write classical music, either. I'd need to have been dead several hundred years . . .

Zoë Well, what do you write?

Jerome I write—modern music.

Zoë Would I know it? I mean, would I have heard any? Only it would be nice to tell people when I get home—that's if I get home—I met *the* Mr Watkins.

Jerome Jerome.

Zoë Jerome, right. *The* Jerome. Do call me Zoë.

Jerome Tell your friends that if they remember those baby-powder commercials they showed two or three years ago, ten times a night, every night for about eight months—then you met the man who wrote that music and wished to God he hadn't.

Zoë What you mean the—the one with the singing babies?

Jerome nods wearily

(*Excitedly*) All those sweet little singing babies? But that was absolutely brilliant. Did you do the music for that? But that was absolutely fantastic. That was wonderful. That was so clever. That was completely and utterly *brilliant*. You're an absolute genius.

Jerome Thank you.

Zoë Oh, I wish they'd bring that back. It was so good. Brilliant. Gosh. I'm very impressed. What else have you written?

Jerome About three hundred other pieces.

Zoë Any more with singing babies?

Jerome No, no. No more singing babies.

Zoë What else?

Jerome (*wearily*) Three string quartets. An unaccompanied cello sonata. Several pieces for synthesizer . . .

Zoë No, I don't know any of those. Tell me, I bet everybody asks you this—how did you get all those babies singing in tune?

Jerome looks at her incredulously

Or is that a closely guarded secret?

Jerome Yes. I'm afraid it's very—closely guarded.

Zoë (*disappointed*) Oh. Brilliant, anyway.

Jerome (*without malice*) Would you describe yourself as an intelligent person?

Zoë Me?

Jerome Yes.

Zoë Heavens! I don't know. As an actress friend of mine used to say—it depends on the script, dear. (*She laughs*)

Jerome (*nodding*) Yes. That's a good point. That's a very good point.

Zoë It's an intellectual role this then, is it?

Jerome No. Just reasonably intelligent. I was just wondering——

Zoë Oh, I can come over as pretty clever, you know. I did Arkadina in *The Seagull*—do you know it?

Jerome No.

Zoë Chekhov. I mean she's often played as quite stupid but I don't think she is. Of course, I was much too young for her . . . (*Pause*) Shall I walk around again for you?

Jerome No.

Zoë restlessly walks about

Zoë And I played the wife in *See How They Run*. She's no fool, either. (*Pause. At the console, pretending to play a keyboard*) Diddly-diddly diddly dom. Is this where you compose?

Jerome Uh-huh.

Zoë Brilliant. What is it?

Jerome It's a digital audio system.

Zoë Ah-ha!

Jerome Which I use primarily for sampling and synthesizing aural sounds.

Zoë Brilliant. Whey-hey. Diddly-diddly——

Jerome Please don't touch anything. Please.

Zoë No, no. Sorry. I promise.

Nan comes through busily with a bundle of dirty sheets en route to the kitchen, humming to herself

What on earth is it doing?

Jerome Oh, she'll do that for hours. It keeps her happy.

Zoë Oh. (*She studies the console; reading*) What do "bedroom one", "bedroom two" and "bathroom" mean?

Jerome Just an experiment.

Zoë Something you were composing?

Jerome That's right.
Zoë A bathroom suite. (*She laughs*)
Jerome (*meaning her laugh*) Very good, very good.
Zoë Pretty good for me. (*She laughs again*) I very rarely make jokes.
Jerome Jokes?
Zoë Just then. I made a joke. Didn't you ...? Oh, you meant the laugh? You liked the laugh?
Jerome (*rising*) Very good. Excellent.
Zoë Thank you. I'll put that on my CV. (*Scowling*) When I get some more done. Special skills include laughing.
Jerome Let me show you something ...

Jerome goes to the console and starts the video recording he has located earlier. In a moment, the screen lights up. A young girl of about nine appears on the screen. Conventionally pretty, fair-haired and slightly self-conscious

Young Geain Hallo, Daddy. This is Geain. I'm just calling to say thank you very much for all my presents. They were all really live. Especially the disc voucher which I'm going to spend on the new Jamie Butterscotch and one by The Grind. Mummy gave me a long dress which is really live. It's yellow and grey and Granny and Grandpa gave me some live jewellery to go with it and I'm going to wear that tonight because we're going out to dinner to Del—to Del something—I can't remember. I wish you were coming, Daddy. And I miss you very much. And I hope to see you soon. Bye. Love from Geain. (*She makes a big cross in the air with her finger*) That's a kiss.

Jerome stops the tape and looks at Zoë who realizes she is supposed to comment

Zoë That's your daughter?
Jerome Yes.
Zoë Lovely.
Jerome Thank you.

Slight pause

Zoë I couldn't play her.
Jerome Oh, no ...
Zoë You don't want that?
Jerome No.
Zoë Oh, good. (*Pause*) How old is she?
Jerome Geain? She'll be thirteen.
Zoë Thirteen? She looks quite young for her age.
Jerome Oh, that was recorded—some time ago.
Zoë I see.
Jerome That was probably the last occasion I was permitted to see her.
Zoë Really?
Jerome Her mother—my wife wouldn't let her phone me after that. She wouldn't let me visit her. She wouldn't let Geain visit me.
Zoë Why not?

Jerome Why not? Because my wife is a selfish, vindictive, unforgiving bitch.
Zoë Oh, I see. Yes. (*A pause*) Do you want me to play her, then?
Jerome (*angrily*) No, I don't want you to play her.
Zoë No, right. Sorry, sorry.

Nan comes through again with the same bundle of sheets, bound for the bedroom once more

I think I'd better go and give her a hand in a minute.

She laughs feebly. Jerome is silent again

It's a nice name, Jane. *Jane Eyre*. We did that one. I played the mad Mrs Rochester. Behind the panelling. Not much of a part. I should have played Jane, really. I'd have been really good.
Jerome G-E-A-I-N.
Zoë Sorry?
Jerome Ours is spelt G-E-A-I-N. At her mother's insistence.
Zoë How unusual. What is it? Gaelic?
Jerome No, just pretentious.
Zoë I'd love to have children of my own. Well, for about twenty minutes, anyway. Sometimes I think, wouldn't it be lovely to hear them rushing about the flat, laughing and yelling? And then—at about six in the morning I think, no, it wouldn't at all, I can't think of anything worse. But I suppose with the right man—someone who'd share them—do all the cleaning up—possibly they'd be everything I ever wanted. But I doubt it. I suppose you're either maternal or you aren't. I know which I am.
Jerome (*who has been staring at her, coming to a sudden decision*) All right. We'll give it a try. The proposition is this. I want you to live here with me for twenty-four hours as my loving, caring companion——
Zoë Ah, now, listen, I thought we'd been through all that——
Jerome In just about a week's time, my wife and my daughter, together with some—petty official from the Social Services—are coming here, to this flat, for the first time in four years. And between them, my wife and this official will decide whether or not they consider this a fit place and, more important, whether they consider me a fit person for her to spend time with in the future. On their one visit everything rests. If I fail to meet their high standards of homeliness and hygiene, then it's unlikely I shall be allowed to see my daughter again.
Zoë Unless you visit her.
Jerome Visit her? Where?
Zoë Where she lives.
Jerome She lives with my wife. How can I visit there? The woman loathes the sight of me.
Zoë She's coming here, though.
Jerome She's coming here to make damn sure she prevents any future visit by Geain. I've told you, Corinna is a very vindictive, unforgiving woman.
Zoë Unforgiving of what?
Jerome (*evasively*) Unforgiving of—anything you care to mention.
Zoë So you need to present them with a solid domestic front.

Jerome I want to present them with a relationship that's so perfect that not only can she not find fault with it, but it doubles her up with jealousy. It leaves her eating her heart out with envy and frustration.

Zoë Yes. (*Tentatively*) If you don't mind my saying so—it's beginning to sound a wee bit vindictive on both sides——

Jerome How do you mean?

Zoë Well . . .

Jerome I have cause. I have cause to be vindictive . . .

Zoë Oh, yes. Only——

Jerome (*excitedly*) She's not the one who's been forbidden to see her own daughter. Denied all those precious moments watching her child grow up. She's not the one who's been left to live alone in an empty flat. Unable to work—unable to write a single note of music for four years. Four years!

Zoë (*alarmed*) Yes.

Jerome Nothing.

Zoë No.

Jerome And you talk about me being vindictive. (*Turning on her, angrily*) Whose side are you on? You're taking her side and you haven't even met her . . .

Zoë No, I'm not. Honestly, I'm not——

Jerome Do you want this job or don't you?

Zoë Yes, yes . . .

Jerome Because if you don't, I can quite easily . . .

Zoë No, I do. I want it very much. I do honestly. Please, please, please!

A silence. Jerome simmers down

Jerome (*muttering*) God, you bloody women. You don't half stick together, don't you?

Zoë Not really.

Jerome My sister, right or wrong. Yes?

Zoë Not at all. Don't be . . .

Jerome What? Don't be what?

Zoë (*changing tack*) I think I could be the perfect female companion. For twenty-four hours, anyway. I think I could do that. Not much longer though. Mind you, my ex-boyfriend would claim I couldn't even manage it for twenty-four hours. (*Expansively*) Hallo! Welcome! Welcome! Welcome!

Jerome (*anxiously*) Yes, I don't want anything too . . .

Zoë No, well, I'll work on it. Do you think I should wear glasses? Do you think it's a glasses part?

Jerome No, I don't.

Zoë No. Still, I need something. I always need some little thing to start off with. Some actors always start with the shoes. (*Gazing at her feet*) I don't think I'll start with these, somehow. I can do quite a deep voice. Shall I give her a deep voice? Like this?

Jerome (*alarmed by her enthusiasm*) No, no, please. Just your normal voice. Just be your normal self. Please.

Zoë (*calming down*) OK. I could do the limp like that thing out there . . . (*She mimics Nan's walk*) No, only joking. Well, OK. I accept.

Jerome Good.

Zoë Actually, it's quite handy me being stuck here. I mean, it gives me a chance to research, you know. Talk to you. Find out what constitutes your perfect mate.

Jerome So long as we convince them.

Zoë Oh, yes. Only it helps if I don't pour you a large Scotch when you're a teetotaller. Those sort of things tend to give the game away. (*Pause*) Or cooking you chicken when you're a vegetarian. (*Finding the burnt tinfoil dish*) Or baking home-made cakes when you're on a diet . . . Is this one of those new self-cooking dishes?

Jerome That's right.

Zoë How was it?

Jerome Delicious.

Zoë (*doubtfully examining the burnt dish*) Yes. (*Pause*) Talking of food and drink. Would it sound awful . . .? Only I did start out very early this morning. And my ex-boyfriend had polished off the muesli.

Jerome Oh yes, certainly, I'll see what we have. I've just stocked up, there's quite a bit of frozen stuff.

Zoë No, I'll do it. Don't bother.

Jerome That's OK, I'll . . .

Zoë No, no, please. Let me. Start getting into the role. Little woman in kitchen. (*She starts for the kitchen, then stops*) Where's the thing?

Jerome In the bedroom.

Zoë OK. Watch this then. A startling character transformation.

Zoë marches out to the kitchen

Jerome watches her rather apprehensively

She comes straight back again

I'm sorry, I'm not going in there. My God, what have you been doing?

Jerome What?

Zoë It's *disgusting* out there. It's *revolting*. It's swimming in—yuurrrk. Uggh! Ugghh! It's your ghastly machine. It must be.

Jerome She does—spill things.

Zoë Spill things? She's tipped whole piles of festering food all over everything. You should be dead, you know. It's a miracle you're alive . . . I tell you, that machine is a——

Jerome All right, I'll do it.

Zoë I'm not eating *anything* from there——

Jerome It's instant stuff. It's sealed. I'll just put it in the oven.

Zoë Well, make sure we open it in here . . .

Jerome Whatever you say.

He goes out to the kitchen

Zoë, left alone, decides to practise her role. She takes up the stance of a beaming hostess

Zoë (*brightly*) Hallo! Hallo! Hallo! Welcome! Welcome! Welcome! Sorry. I completely lost track of the time. Typical. (*Turning as if hearing someone calling*) What's that? Just a tick, darling. I'm coming, darling.

As she is doing this, Nan comes from the bedrooms. She has finally got rid of the sheets. She is heading towards the hall. But she sees Zoë and stops, staring at her impassively

(*Seeing Nan*) Oh, hallo, I was just . . .

Nan moves off to the hall and goes out

Mind your own business, anyway.

She is about to start again when the phone rings

Jerome (*off*) Leave that. It'll go on to answer.

Zoë waits. Lupus appears on the screen after the phone has rung a couple of times. He is seated at a drum kit which he has set up around his video machine. We can see part of this. He is slightly more wild-eyed than before and possibly suffering from the effects of some stimulant. Zoë stares at him incredulously

Lupus (*from the video*) Hiya, Jerry. I seem to have got the old answering machine again—but on the offchance you're there and would like to register as the only person left in the world who is still prepared to talk to me, here I am. Calling on my final life raft, my only friend, my single ray of hope in the dark endless tunnel some of us laughingly refer to as life. I'm afraid it's down to you, Jerry. You stand between one man and the end of his tether. His final straw. His last burning bridge.

Under this, Jerome returns from the kitchen with two packets

Jerome Do you want Breast of Grouse en Croûte or Gourmet Chicken with Almonds and Wild Strawberry Sauce?
Zoë (*not inspired by either*) Grouse.
Jerome There is Sliced Beef in Clam Sauce.
Zoë Grouse.
Jerome OK. I think I'll try this chicken.
Zoë There's an extraordinary man on your phone in a desperate state.
Jerome Yes, I know. It takes twenty seconds. Can you wait?

Jerome goes off to the kitchen

Lupus has been going under this

Lupus You may have gathered that my wife has gone. My son has gone. Our furniture has gone. Everything. But for the last time, Jerry. Whoever she's with this time, she can stay with him. I'm not letting her back in. Not this time. She chose to leave, by the way, whilst I went for a job which incidentally I never got. The dynamic geriatric Finchley tea-dance trio decided they could manage without me. Their Arts Council grant came through and they celebrated by buying a drum machine. (*He laughs heartily and mirthlessly*) So, here we are, sitting amongst this load of obsolete gear (*smashes a cymbal*)—that nobody wants—(*hits a drum*)—

why hear the real thing when you can hear a synthesized mock-up—
(*another whack of a cymbal*)—I thought you might like to hear it, Jerry,
before I burn it all—the last live drum solo, as played by man. The very
last.

Jerome returns. He holds a cloth round the two now very hot tinfoil dishes

*Zoë, who has been watching the screen transfixed, springs up. Lupus is
preparing himself to start a drum solo*

Jerome Look out, they're hot.
Zoë Sorry, I'll—clear some space . . . There's this extraordinary man. Is he
all right?
Jerome (*dismissively*) Yes, he's fine. He's always like that.

Lupus starts to play the drums

Oh, for God's sake. Lupus!

*Jerome dives for the console and turns down the volume. Lupus thrashes away
silently for some minutes under the next*

Hang on. I'll get some cutlery.

Zoë gives him a look

I'll wash it first, don't worry.

*Jerome goes out. Nan has entered, holding the nozzle of a vacuum cleaner
but unattached to any machine. She stops behind Zoë*

Zoë (*calling to Jerome*) I think I'd feel happier if you could boil everything
before I touch it, please.
Nan (*quietly and venomously*) Making ourselves comfortable, are we,
Deborah?
Zoë (*jumping round in alarm*) What?
Nan I know what you're after, dear, and you're not going to have him. If
you want Jerome, the only way you're going to get him is over my dead
body, you calculating little trollop.
Zoë (*very indignant*) I beg your pardon.
Nan You'd better watch your step, Deborah darling, or one of these nights
you're going to wake up with your throat cut.

Nan moves away and goes off to the bedrooms

Zoë stares at her in horror. She clutches her throat

Jerome returns with some knives and forks and two tins of beer

Jerome Here.
Zoë (*recoiling*) Ah!
Jerome You OK?
Zoë Yes—it was—hot.
Jerome Good. I brought some beer. I thought you'd prefer the can rather
than our glasses. (*He opens both the meals*) That's yours. I think.

Zoë Thank you.
Jerome (*examining his own dish*) Yes, I think these must be the wild
strawberries. Do you want beer?
Zoë Please.

Jerome opens the beers

Jerome Go ahead, do start. Before it gets rusty.

She tries it

Zoë Mmm! Not bad.
Jerome Hot enough?
Zoë Perfect.

They eat

How long were you married? To Corinna?
Jerome Eleven years.
Zoë God. A lifetime. Must have felt very strange. Splitting up.
Jerome Yes.
Zoë I mean, even if you loathed the sight of each other.
Jerome Yes.
Zoë Was she a musician?
Jerome Corinna? (*He laughs*) No. She was my bank manager. Until I
moved my account.
Zoë Do you miss her?
Jerome No.
Zoë Would you ever consider going back to her?
Jerome Look, what the hell is this? A census?
Zoë I just want to know. I need to know.
Jerome Why? Why do you want to know all that?
Zoë Because I'll need to. If I'm to behave like someone who's been living
with you for some time, I'll need to know.
Jerome Well, you don't need to know all that. I'll tell you what you need to
know, don't worry.
Zoë OK. Fine. Fire ahead.

A pause

Jerome (*grumpily*) What do you want to know?
Zoë No, no. I'm not asking any more questions. You tell me.
Jerome It's all right . . .
Zoë No, if I ask questions you just bite my head off. You can tell me, go on.
Jerome I'm sorry. I—I haven't really talked to anyone—well, not face to
face—for some time, you see. Since they fully automated the hypermar-
ket, I don't think I've spoken to anyone for months. So, you'll have to
make allowances.
Zoë I understand.
Jerome So. If you want to ask questions. Please.
Zoë Right.

They eat

Jerome Go ahead.

Zoë I will. I'm just trying to think of some. Why did your wife leave you?

Jerome I don't think that's any of your damn business.

Zoë Oh, terrific ... Forget it. I'll just make it up. I'll make it all up. Just don't blame me if it all goes totally wrong. When it turns out that I don't know vital facts about you that I should know——

Jerome I just don't see that you need to——

Zoë Look. If it transpires that your wife left you because for eleven years— or whatever it was—you drove her absolutely mad whistling in the nude at breakfast time—then that's something I ought to know. Because it just might crop up in conversation between the two of us. "Darling, doesn't he drive you mad the way he whistles in the nude at breakfast?" "No, not at all, dear, I love it, I find it totally refreshing ..."

Jerome All right, all right. My wife left me because ... She claimed I drove her mad ...

Zoë Whistling in the nude at breakfast ...? Sorry.

Jerome She wasn't, in the end, prepared to live with a creative person. That's what it boiled down to. She wasn't prepared to fit in with the lifestyle of a creative entity. Such as myself. That's all. I'm not saying she was a selfish woman. Nor am I saying she was a woman who refused to adapt or even begin to understand the pressures that—a creative person can undergo. I'm not saying that about her. After all, why should she? She's just a bloody bank manager.

Zoë (*sympathetically*) No. And you probably didn't understand a lot about banking, did you?

Jerome (*sharply*) What's that got to do with it?

Zoë (*quickly*) Nothing.

Jerome Still, I'm sure she'll make some—chief clerk—a very good wife.

Zoë (*deciding this isn't a line worth pursuing further*) I'd love to hear some of your music. Could I, possibly?

Jerome Yes. Perhaps. Sometime. As I say, I haven't written anything for— ages.

Zoë Since they left?

Jerome Nearly.

Zoë Four years. Heavens. You really did need them, then, in some ways? Well, your muse did.

Jerome Geain. I needed Geain. I need her back more than anything in the world.

Zoë, for the first time, notices the signs of his inner distress

Zoë (*moved*) Well, I'll—do my best for you. (*Pause*) Did she inspire your Singing Babies? I bet she did.

Jerome *First Sounds*. Yes. (*Pause*) I recorded her over several days ...

Zoë You mean it was actually her? Actually Geain you used?

Jerome Yes. That was the first occasion I started using purely natural sounds—sampling and treating them. It took months.

Zoë Fancy. And all that for what? Thirty seconds?

Jerome Thirty seconds? It was a forty-five-minute piece originally.

Zoë Oh, I see. There's more?
Jerome Much, much, much more.
Zoë You can't write at all, then? No ideas?
Jerome I know what I want to write. But I don't know how to do it.
Zoë What?
Jerome (*more to himself*) I know what it's going to be. I know what I want
to say. It's how to say it. I haven't got the sound. I haven't heard it. Three
years and I'm still waiting to hear the sound.
Zoë What do you want to say?
Jerome I want to say—what I want to say is—well, I want to say—love.
Really.
Zoë (*mystified*) Love?
Jerome Yes.
Zoë I see. What sort of love?
Jerome Just—generally. Love. You know ...
Zoë (*puzzled*) No, I'm not sure I——
Jerome (*tetchily*) Love. You've heard of love, I presume?
Zoë Yes, yes. Sorry, only you're not putting it awfully well.
Jerome (*irritably*) Of course I'm not putting it awfully well. If I could put it
awfully well, there wouldn't be a problem. I want to express the feeling of
love in an abstract musical form. In such a way that anyone who hears
it—*anyone*—no matter what language they speak—no matter what creed
or colour—they will recognize it—and respond to it—and relate it to their
own feelings of love that they have or they've experienced at some time—
so they say—yes, my God, that's it! That's what it is! And maybe who
knows, consequently, there might be a bit more of it.

Zoë is spellbound by this

Zoë How wonderful. (*She reflects for a second*) It must have been a bit like
this, sitting with Beethoven.
Jerome I doubt it.
Zoë That's how I imagine it, anyway.
Jerome I don't think Beethoven sat down all that much. He used to stamp
about the place, shouting.
Zoë There you are, then. You're both terribly similar.

Pause. They have both finished their meal

Oh, it must be just so awful for you. Having all those ideas and not being
able to express them. Poor you.

Jerome looks at her

I mean, I know sort of how you feel. I get that way if I'm just writing a
letter. I want to say something really—I don't know—heartfelt to
someone. And it all comes out like the inside of some awful Christmas
card. Happy tidings, boyfriend dear. At this joyous time of year. When
what you mean to say is: I love you incredibly much and I'd do just about
everything I could in the world to make you happy and I just want to be
with you and stay close to you for ever and ever and ever ... And you try

and write that down so it makes sense and what do you get? Happy
tidings, boyfriend dear ... (*Aware of his gaze*) What's the matter?
Jerome Nothing.
Zoë Are you having second thoughts?
Jerome No. Third thoughts.
Zoë (*slightly apprehensive*) Oh? What are those?
Jerome I was just thinking—you're a very nice person, really. Only, saying
it like that, I think I sound rather like one of your Christmas cards.

A pause. Zoë is a little ill at ease

Zoë I think I'll sing my song for you now, if you don't mind.
Jerome (*rather dismayed*) Really?
Zoë Well, it's either that or my Shakespeare. And I don't think Queen
Margaret would go down frightfully well after chicken and strawberries.
(*Arranging herself*) It's all right, it's quite short ... (*Making a false start*)
You're not my—— Hang on. (*She sorts out her first note*) Right. Here we
go.

> (*Singing*) You're not my first love ...
> It would only be a lie if I pretended—
> In the past there have been others
> Who have slept between these covers
> But I promise
> Though you're far too late in life to be my first love,
> You'll be my last love.
> I swear to you, you're gonna be my last love ...

She finishes her song. Silence

Well. It has this great accompaniment. Diddly-diddly diddly dom.

*She smiles at him awkwardly. Jerome rises and moves to her. He stands by her,
then kisses her. They break and stare at each other*

You taste of wild strawberries.
Jerome You taste of grouse.

Zoë laughs. Jerome smiles one of his rare smiles

Do you want any more?
Zoë More?
Jerome Food?
Zoë No.
Jerome Any more anything of anything?
Zoë (*without hesitation*) Yes, please.
Jerome Well, shall we ...? What would you prefer to do? I mean, would
you like to—here? Or ...?
Zoë I don't mind. Here's fine if—you ...
Jerome Or there's the bedroom, that might be ...
Zoë Sure. That's fine. Will she have made the bed by now, do you think?
(*She laughs*)
Jerome Oh, no, that's no problem. Those sheets were just for her to——

Zoë Well, fine. Shall we go in there?
Jerome (*unmoving*) Yes, yes, yes.
Zoë You want to?
Jerome Oh, yes. You bet.
Zoë I mean, we don't have to if you——?
Jerome No, no, no . . . (*Laughing*) Useful research, whatever else . . .
Zoë (*drawing back, concerned*) Oh, I wasn't . . . just for that.
Jerome No, no. I was joking.
Zoë I mean, I really want to. I don't—if I don't want to . . . I don't do that sort of thing.
Jerome I know, I'm sure. Nor do I.
Zoë Good. (*Pause*) Well—shall we . . .?
Jerome Why not?

They both move towards the bedrooms

As they do, Nan enters clasping the section of vacuum cleaner

Zoë jumps

Nan passes them, crosses to the hall and goes out

She's OK.
Zoë I wonder. Would you think it awful of me—if I asked you to switch it off?
Jerome Switch her off?
Zoë Just while we were—just while we were in . . .
Jerome It's not very good for her, to keep switching her on and off, you see . . .
Zoë No, no, I'm sure. It's just if it did happen to come in while we were—I think I'd probably scream or something . . .
Jerome Well, I could disengage her. That would put her on standby. I'd disconnect her movement functions but leave her brain working . . .
Zoë (*not wanting the details*) Yes, fine. That sounds fine. I wouldn't want to damage her.
Jerome (*calling*) Nan, here.
Nan (*off*) Coming, Nan.

Nan enters from the hall

Zoë Did that face come with it? I mean, is that how it came out of the factory?
Jerome No, I—tinkered around with it. You can easily alter it, you just heat it first with a hair drier.
Zoë Well, I think you could have chosen a better face. It looks like Mrs Danvers.
Jerome Nan, sit.
Nan Sitting, Nan. (*She sits*)
Jerome Nan, Function Command Jerome Disengage.

Nan gives a slight beep

Nan Disengaged.

Jerome Nan, walk.

She gives a little beep and a twitch but stays in the chair

(*Trying again*) Nan, walk.

Nan beeps and twitches again but stays still

There you are, you see. Can't move at all.

Zoë No. (*She seems a little guilty at what she's requested Jerome to do*)

Jerome I'll just check—things are off.

He goes to the console. He checks, unseen by Zoë, his recording machines. Zoë stands in the doorway, waiting for him. Nan's head turns slowly and looks at her

Zoë Ah!

Jerome What is it?

Zoë She's just moved her head.

Jerome Well, yes, she can still move her head. That's all right, isn't it?

Zoë Oh yes, that's quite all right. I just wasn't expecting it. (*She starts fumbling under her dress*)

Jerome (*watching her*) Are you all right?

Zoë (*having difficulty*) Yes, I was—I was just going to show you my—show you my ... (*She produces a string of plastic credit-type cards from her thigh wallet*) There. Better get it over with. (*Pointing to one green card in particular among the string of others*) My Green Card. OK?

Jerome Oh, yes ...

Zoë I had a full check. Last month. I'm all clear. CBH One.

Jerome Fine. Good. Congratulations.

Zoë Well. You can't be too careful. Can you?

Jerome No.

Slight pause

Zoë Are you ...? Have you got ...?

Jerome Oh, yes—somewhere. It's in the ... I put it in the ... It's around ...

Zoë (*slightly doubtful*) Good. (*Making to move*) Well ...

Jerome After you.

Zoë Thank you. (*As she goes*) You still want to do this, don't you?

Zoë goes into the bedroom

Jerome (*switching off the lights and following her*) Oh, yes ... You bet. Rather.

Jerome goes into the bedroom

Zoë (*off*) Because if you don't, I shan't be hurt ...

Jerome (*off*) Oh, I do. I do. Do you?

Zoë (*off*) Oh, yes ... You bet.

The bedroom door closes and their voices are cut off. Nan sits alone. She is lit, primarily from the console lights which start blinking and flashing in response to the unheard sounds in the bedroom. The light patterns become increasingly vigorous

Nan (*slowly and with difficulty*) Deb-or-rah . . . Deb-or-rah . . .

The lights continue to flicker on her face

Black-out

Scene 2

A few hours later. It is probably morning, though it's impossible to tell

Nan has gone. Jerome sits on the stool which is swivelled to one side of the console. He is working at a stretch of keyboard. He is wearing headphones, so there is no sound. He grunts occasionally to himself as he works

Nan swings in from the kitchen with another of her upside-down mugs of coffee. She puts it down near Jerome

Nan Nice cup of cocoa. Don't let it get cold, now.

Jerome, even if he hears her, ignores her he is so absorbed

> *Nan returns to the kitchen. After a moment, Zoë, rather crumpled from sleep, comes from the bedroom wrapped in a blanket. She watches Jerome for a moment. She moves behind him and kisses the top of his head gently*

Jerome (*rather loudly because of his headphones*) Nan, stop! Stop that at once.

Zoë pulls back, hurt. Jerome realizes belatedly that it was unlikely to have been Nan. He turns and takes off the headphones

Zoë Good-morning.
Jerome Good-morning.
Zoë How long have you been up?
Jerome (*shrugging*) Oh . . .
Zoë I've slept for hours.
Jerome Yes . . .
Zoë Well . . .
Jerome Yes . . .
Zoë (*kissing him*) Good-morning.
Jerome Morning.

Zoë stands smiling at him. He seems rather embarrassed. There is a characteristic crash from the kitchen

Zoë (*drily*) Mrs Danvers is up bright and early, I hear.
Jerome Well, she's got a busy day ahead.
Zoë I'm glad she didn't bring me early-morning tea.
Jerome She's been known to. It's not an experience worth repeating. By the way, we had a visit from Rita. It's all fixed.
Zoë Thank goodness.

Jerome The Daughters have agreed your fine. Five hundred pounds.

Zoë (*aghast*) Five hundred pounds!

Jerome It was either that or fifty lashes. I said you'd prefer the fine.

Zoë Well, the Blaise Gillespie Agency is footing the bill for that, I can tell
you. They should have warned me.

Jerome You'll need this. (*He picks up a grubby coloured card and hands it to
her*) It's your pass card. To get you back to the railway station.

Zoë (*reading*) "This is to—certify—I the undersigned have paid my debt to
society." Oh, really.

Jerome Yes, you have to sign it, too. Don't lose it.

Zoë I'd be a lot more impressed if they could spell "certify". (*She puts the
card down*)

Jerome I'll come with you. See you off. If you'd like me to. Do you want
anything? Tea or anything?

Zoë No. I must get dressed. I need to be back by midday. I've got an
audition. It's a new musical. Set in a women's prison. *Hooray for
Holloway*—well, that's what everyone's calling it, anyway. I think I'll do
my song for them. What do you think?

Jerome Sure. Why not?

Zoë seems reluctant to move. They stare at each other

I—don't know what to say, really.

Zoë I—was wondering. Whether I should be coming back? Whether you'd
like me to come back again? I mean, sooner than—like this evening? Or
tomorrow? We've still got a lot to discuss, haven't we? If we're going to
get everything right for this meeting with your wife? And your daughter?
What do you think? I mean, I'm not trying to push. Just as you like. What
do you say?

A silence

I don't mind. Only do say something. Please.

Jerome kisses her gently

Is that a yes?

Jerome Is that what you'd like?

Zoë Yes.

Jerome Then, that's what I'd like.

Zoë Good. (*Pause*) Just one thing.

Jerome What?

Zoë Who the hell is Deborah?

Jerome (*startled*) Who?

Zoë Deborah. Who is she?

Jerome No idea at all. Never heard of her.

Zoë Well. Somebody has, that's all I can say. Mrs Danvers keeps muttering
her name at me every time she passes.

Jerome I can't think why she'd do that.

Zoë No, right. I must just remind her of something she used to know. Her
old pal, Debbie, the deep freezer perhaps. (*She watches him for a second*)

Last night, was that the first time you—you hadn't made love to anyone for some time, had you?

Jerome Three years.

Zoë (*not unkindly*) Well, you'll soon get the hang of it again, I'm sure. (*Realizing she may have put this rather badly*) So. I'll get dressed. OK?

Jerome Yes. (*He plays with some of the knobs on the console*)

Zoë You all right?

Jerome Yes.

Zoë What were you doing? You weren't composing something, were you?

Jerome Not really. I—er . . . (*He waves his hand at the console and presses a start button. From the speakers a fragment of a composition that he has been working on. It is, recognizably, Zoë's laugh, recorded, sampled and re-treated in a simple, gentle, melodic line*)

Zoë (*recognizing herself*) Is that me?

Jerome Yes.

They listen. It is quite short. It finishes. Jerome stops the machine

Zoë That was me.

Jerome That's right.

Zoë When did you do that?

Jerome While you were asleep.

Zoë But when did you record me? Yesterday?

Jerome That's right.

Zoë You secretly recorded my laugh? My awful laugh?

Jerome It's a very nice laugh.

Zoë Watch it. I shall demand repeat fees. (*She smiles*) It's very good.

Jerome (*smiling*) Thank you. It's a sketch at the moment.

Zoë Terribly clever. It's all done with that machine?

Jerome Yes.

Zoë Brilliant. Brilliant machine. I'll tell you something, do you think when it goes—(*she hums a few notes*)—it wouldn't be better if it went—(*she demonstrates something different*)—don't you think?

Jerome (*guardedly*) How do you mean?

Zoë Like—(*she hums her improvement again*).

Jerome It doesn't go—(*he hums her improvement*).

Zoë I know it doesn't. It goes—(*she hums her version of the original*).

Jerome No, it doesn't go—(*he hums her version of the original*). It goes—(*he hums the original*).

Zoë Well—(*she hums the original*)—then. I still think it would be better if it went—(*she hums her improvement*).

Jerome No, it wouldn't.

Zoë It would.

Jerome It wouldn't.

Zoë Why not?

Jerome Because it doesn't go like that. That's not the way it goes.

Zoë I know it doesn't. I'm saying, perhaps it should.

Jerome (*angry now*) No, it shouldn't. It goes the way it goes because it goes that way——

Zoë Why? Why does it, necessarily?

Jerome (*yelling*) Because that's the way it goes, that's why. Because I wrote it that way and I'm the one that matters.

Zoë (*defensively*) All right! Yes! (*A pause*) There's no need to shout at me. I'm not your machine, you know.

Jerome (*muttering*) At least she doesn't try and rewrite my music for me.

Zoë I'm sorry. I thought you might like a suggestion. Obviously you don't. Fine. (*Pause*) Obviously, you think that's perfect. Fine. You're the expert.

Jerome (*testily*) Right.

Nan comes from the kitchen to the hall carrying a floor-mop handle without the mop attached. She goes out busily

Zoë stares

It's her day to mop the hall.

Zoë Oh, good. I'm sure that floor could really do with a good scrape. Is that all you've done, then?

Jerome What?

Zoë Just that bit? Is that all you've written?

Jerome No.

Zoë Oh.

Jerome I started a second sketch.

Zoë Good. (*Pause*) Well, let's hear it then. I won't say a word, I won't say a word, I promise.

Jerome (*reluctantly*) It's not finished.

He plays her the second sketch. It is, like the first, based on Zoë but is very different in mood—obviously this time based on a recording of Zoë's love sounds. She listens thunderstruck. It finishes. Jerome switches off the machine again

Zoë Is that what I think it is?

Jerome Yes.

Zoë You recorded that while we were . . .?

Jerome Yes.

Zoë I don't believe it. You mean, while we were making love you just calmly leant out of bed and switched on a tape recorder?

Jerome No . . .

Zoë No wonder you didn't seem to have your mind on the job . . .

Jerome Of course I didn't.

Zoë Then how else did you . . .?

Jerome I didn't switch it on specially. They're on all the time.

Zoë All the time?

Jerome Yes.

Zoë What, you mean like now?

Jerome Yes. All the time.

Zoë What, everywhere? In the—everywhere?

Jerome I keep saying. Yes.

Zoë (*aghast*) You're sick. You're diseased. You're perverted . . .

Jerome That's the way I work—that's how I work.

Zoë Well, I'm sorry, that's not the way I work. You switch that thing off right now or I'm leaving.

Jerome I can't switch it off. Look, it has to be on, don't you see? What's recorded here is—is what I use later. Some of it. Not all of it, obviously.

Zoë Then you can just record parts ...

Jerome How do I know which parts to record? Jesus——

Zoë Well, I can tell you the parts you're not going to record. You are not recording me making love, me having a bath or me in the loo—that's three for a start ... My God, did you do this sort of thing to your wife? To your daughter?

Jerome Yes.

Zoë Didn't they mind? Yes, of course they minded, they walked out on you. What about Deborah, what did she have to say?

Jerome (*shouting*) For the tenth time, I don't know any Deborah!

A loud crash from the hall

Zoë Well, somebody evidently does. Why don't you ask old Mrs Danvers about her?

She stamps off to the bedroom. Nan comes from the hall, almost immediately

Nan I know what you're after, dear, and you're not going to have him. If you want Jerome, the only way you're going to get him——

Jerome Nan, stop!

Nan Stop, Nan.

Jerome stares after Zoë

Nan goes out to the kitchen with her mop handle

Jerome slides up a fader on the desk. Zoë's voice in the bedroom can be heard coming over the speakers

Zoë's voice ... never known anything so sick in my life ... it's disgusting ... I mean, there is such a thing as basic privacy ... just to record someone without even ... I mean, recording us when we were ... If you're recording this now, Jerome, which I presume you must be—when you play this back I want you to know that you are a sick, twisted voyeur ... or whatever the listening equivalent is ... an auditeur ... a Listening Tom ...

The sounds of her moving out of the bedroom. Jerome hastily fades down the bedroom mike. Zoë is heard approaching. She is finishing fastening the clothes she borrowed

Zoë enters

Zoë I was just saying, you are a Listening Tom.

Jerome I don't know why you're suddenly behaving like this.

Zoë If you honestly don't know, then that's probably the reason you are living on your own, Jerome.

Jerome What are you talking about?

Zoë I'm sorry to disappoint you but you're going to be very hard pressed, even today, to find any woman prepared to have an affair when she runs the risk of having the thing released later in stereo. (*She makes to go*)

Jerome Don't forget your pass, will you?

Zoë returns for the card, her anger giving way to genuine hurt

Nan comes from the kitchen again and stops in the doorway

Zoë God, I'm so upset, you've no idea. I really cared, you know. Did you know that? Oh, it was only supposed to be a job but I actually genuinely cared about you and your wife and your daughter and your music ... And now, it's all been betrayed ...

Jerome I don't see what difference it makes.

Zoë You can't see that there are things that people say and do with each other that they don't want other people to hear? And if they think that other people are going to be listening, then they just don't say them any more?

Jerome But as an artist my work entirely depends on the fact that I do repeat those things——

Zoë Well, then, pardon the language, but bugger your work. There are some things more important.

Jerome Like what?

Zoë Like me, for one. I am considerably more important than your bloody music, pardon the language. I'm sorry.

Jerome Why? What makes you so bloody important?

Zoë Because I'm a bloody human being, that's why. And if you can't see that, I'm sorry for you. I really am. Jerome—I know you don't like people giving you advice—but if you're still thinking of writing your piece about love, really, I should forget it.

Jerome Thank you so much, I'll bear that in mind.

Zoë I mean it, Jerome. Love? How could you ever possibly, ever, in a million years, conceivably describe something you can't even recognize? (*Indicating the motionless Nan*) If you don't believe me, ask her. Even she knows more about it than you do.

Zoë stamps out

Jerome stares after her. The video screen springs to life as she goes out of the front door. She glares at the camera for a second, pulls a face at it, then slams the front door. The screen blanks

Nan (*starting to move to the hall*) I'm going to clean in here today. Don't get under my feet.

A thought occurs to Jerome. He plays with the controls on the console. Sounds of fast replay

Zoë's recorded voice ... for one. I am considerably more important than your bloody music, pardon the language ...

Jerome spools slightly forward

... but if you're still thinking of writing your piece about love, really, I should forget it.

Jerome's recorded voice Thank you so much, I'll bear that in mind.

Zoë's recorded voice I mean it, Jerome. Love? How could you ever poss——

Jerome stops the tape and spools slightly back again

... it, Jerome. Love? How cou——

He plays the tape again, then winds it back by hand. Then forwards again, then back several times, playing and replaying the single word at various speeds, back and forth

... love ... ev-ol ... l .. o .. v .. e ...

Jerome has a couple more goes, then gives up

Jerome No. Never in a million years. No truth. No sincerity. Nothing.

The phone rings. The screen lights up with the Department of Social Services logo. Jerome stares at the screen dully

Mervyn's voice Mr Watkins, this is Mervyn Bickerdyke from the Department of Child Wellbeing. Calling yet again regarding a proposed meeting. This can't go on, Mr Watkins, it really can't. The time is nine o-three. Please, please, call me ...

Jerome Mr Bickerdyke, I would call you with pleasure, only what would be the point?

Mervyn's voice ... my number is, as ever, on screen. Thank you.

Nan has entered and started to vacuum aimlessly around Jerome's feet, using just the disconnected telescopic tube to do so

Jerome (*irritably*) Nan, give it a rest, please ...

She stops

Nan Think I'll have a little rest.

Nan sits down near Jerome. He regards her

Jerome What do you know about love then, you pile of old junk?

Nan is silent

(*Really for want of anything better to do*) Nan, copy.

Nan Copying.

Jerome Love ...

Nan Love ...

Jerome (*more passionately*) Love!

Nan Love!

Jerome No, love!

Nan No, love!

Jerome (*giving up*) ... useless.

Nan ... useless.

Jerome spools the tape machine idly. He stops and plays it

Zoë's recorded voice ... nice name Jane. *Jane Eyre.* We did that one. I played the mad Mrs Rochester. Behind the panelling. Not much of a part. I should have played Jane, really. I'd have been really good——

Jerome stops the tape

Nan ... nice name, Jane. *Jane Eyre.* We did that one. I played the mad Mrs Rochester. Behind the panelling. Not much of a part. I should have played Jane, really. I'd have been really good——

During this, Jerome looks startled for a moment. Then inspiration strikes him

Jerome Ah! (*He goes to a cupboard under the panel. As he passes, he removes Nan's wig, revealing her silver skull beneath*)
Nan (*echoing him*) Ah!

He takes from the cupboard a rolled bundle which he undoes and lays out carefully on the worktop. A neat row of electrical screwdrivers and spanners, etc., together with an open tobacco tin. Each gleaming like a surgeon's implements. He switches off a few general lights so that the illumination is concentrated around the console. He rolls up his sleeves

Jerome (*softly, to Nan*) Well. What the hell. It's worth a try, that's what I say. (*He selects a slender screwdriver and stands over her*)
Nan (*cheerfully*) Well. What the hell. It's worth a try, that's what I say.

Jerome starts to remove a small grub screw from her temple. A sound as he drops the screw into the tin. The shutters clang several times as missiles strike them from outside, giving the impression of thunder. Jerome labours on, impervious, as——

—the CURTAIN *falls*

ACT II

The same. A week later

In the Black-out, the first thing we see is Lupus's face on the screen. He looks terrible. He appears to be calling from a club, judging from the din in the background. The colour variation in the picture is also quite extreme, veering erratically from one vivid hue to the next

Lupus (*from the screen*) Hallo, Jerry, old mate. Thought I'd roll into view, stick my nose over your horizon there. See how things were. I take it you're out or—busy—or something. I'm calling from the Blue Cockatoo. Thought I might look up one or two of the old gang, for old times' sake. Only there doesn't seem to be anyone here tonight. A bit of a heavy mob round the bar—I hope this phone's working OK, I'm not——

He thumps the unit in front of him, out of our vision. The colour alters abruptly. As he continues, the Lights come up on the room. It is much tidier than when we last saw it. A great effort has been made to turn the place into a suitable home for Geain. Most of the equipment—except the main console— has been covered up. The coffee table is partly laid out for an informal tea party

Jerome comes in from the kitchen. He, too, has made a great effort with his appearance

That any better? Anyway, I'm down here at the old Cockatoo if you feel like a jar. Since I finally lost Deborah, I've been . . . (*Yelling to someone out of view*) Hey, keep it down, fellas. Please? (*He thumps the unit again. His colour changes once more*) Since I finally lost Deborah, I've been pretty near to—— (*In response to someone off screen*) What? What's that? And you yours. Yes . . . (*Back in the phone*) Jesus, who are all these guys? Anyway, as I was saying, since Deborah finally decided to go, I've been on the verge of playing the last waltz, I can tell you . . .

Jerome, as if by reflex, his mind on other things, fades Lupus down on the console. Lupus's image continues to chatter silently, changing colour once or twice more. Finally, he bangs the videophone once too often and the thing blanks out

Jerome (*calling*) Darling!
Zoë's voice (*from the kitchen*) Hallo, darling?
Jerome Darling, what are you doing?
Zoë's voice (*off*) I'm just finishing off in here, darling.
Jerome Darling, come on in, they've arrived.
Zoë's voice (*off*) Right you are, darling. Just a tick.

A moment later and Zoë comes on. Or rather it is Nan made over into a version of Zoë. She looks a good deal like Zoë but still has Nan's distinctive walk—and several of Nan's old mannerisms which emerge from time to time. One improvement Jerome seems to have wrought is that she is carrying a plate of sandwiches the right way up. She, too, is very smartly dressed in the usual long frock and with a great deal of ribbons and bows in her new wig. Jerome has also rather emphasized her figure. She's a degree more voluptuous than Zoë and more shapely than Nan. She looks rather like a parody of an old-style Southern belle

Nan (*brightly, as she enters*) Hallo! Hallo! Hallo! Welcome! Welcome! Welcome! Sorry. I completely lost track of the time. Typical.

She puts the sandwiches down on the coffee table. Jerome watches anxiously

Jerome Good. Good girl. That's it. Darling, will you fetch the tea, or shall I?

Nan I'll fetch the tea, darling. Excuse me.

She goes off

Jerome watches her critically

Jerome (*muttering*) There's nothing I can do with that leg.

Nan (*off, from the kitchen*) Just coming, everyone.

A crash from the kitchen

(*Off*) Oh, for goodness' sake, you extremely stupid old bat. Who put that there, then?

Jerome Oh, for God's sake . . . (*Calling angrily*) Darling!

Nan (*off, sweetly*) Yes, darling.

Jerome Darling, come here, you scrapheap.

Nan (*off*) Coming, darling.

Nan returns, empty-handed

Jerome gets out a small screwdriver from his tool kit

Jerome (*brusquely*) Darling, sit down.

Nan (*sitting*) Sitting down, darling.

Jerome selects a screwdriver and approaches Nan

Jerome (*muttering*) They're going to be here in a minute, you useless heap. Darling, disengage.

Nan beeps and sits immobile in the chair as Jerome lies on his back on the floor and disappears under her skirt

(*Slightly muffled, to himself really*) Sorry to switch you off but I'm not getting a hundred volts through me again. Yes . . . I keep adjusting this balance control but—it's such—fine . . . tuning . . . I think it's this leg of yours—you keep shaking your works about . . . Darling, engage.

Nan beeps again

Nan Reconnected. Operational seventy-eight point seven four. We are twenty-one point two six per cent unstable and are within three point seven four per cent of permanent shutdown.

She beeps. Jerome emerges again

Jerome Don't you dare shut down on me. Not now. Darling, walk about.
Nan Yes, darling. (*She does so*)
Jerome That's better, that's better. Precious!

Nan comes immediately and kisses his cheek. She waltzes away again

 (*An experimental laugh*) Ha! Ha!

Nan responds with one of Zoë's laughs

 Good. (*Calling again*) Precious!

Nan comes and kisses him on the cheek again, then moves away

 Good! Ha! Ha!

Nan laughs again. Jerome moves away to one side of her

 (*In a normal tone*) Zoë . . .

Nan's head turns to look at him, as if listening. She is programmed to do this whenever her name is mentioned. Jerome moves to the other side of her

 (*As before*) Zoë . . .

Nan looks at him again

 (*Rather amazed*) It works. Darling, it works!
Nan It works, darling!
Jerome Nan, still . . .

Nan ignores him

 I mean, darling, still.

Nan stops still

Nan Still, darling.
Jerome Let me straighten your wig. Here . . . (*Studying her*) I don't think I've got your mouth right even now.

He adjusts her appearance, trying to remould her face with his thumbs. The doorbell rings. Jerome jumps. The screen lights up to show Corinna and Mervyn waiting at the front door

 Here we go, then. Darling, kitchen.
Nan Yes, darling. (*She starts to go*)
Jerome No, no. Wait. (*He moves to the console*) Darling, here.
Nan Coming, darling.
Jerome (*standing her in front of the screen where she can study Corinna and Mervyn*) Darling, register.
Nan Register, darling.

Jerome Not child. Not child.
Nan Not child. Registered, Nan.
Jerome Good. Darling, kitchen.
Nan Kitchen, darling.
Jerome Darling, take the plate.
Nan I'll take the plate, darling.

Nan takes up the plate and goes off to the kitchen

Jerome straightens his appearance. The doorbell rings again

Corinna's voice (*impatiently, through the speakers*) Jerome, come on, open the door. Please.
Jerome Here we go. Those warm vibrant tones ...

Jerome presses the door button. They remain out there

Corinna's voice Jerome! For heaven's sake!
Jerome Push the door! Push it!

The doorbell rings again

Mervyn's voice (*from the speakers*) Mr Watkins!
Corinna's voice Jerome!
Jerome Push the bloody thing ...! Oh, for goodness' sake ...

Jerome runs out down the hall

We see, on the video screen, him opening the door to them

Corinna's voice (*from the speakers, sarcastically*) Well, thank you so much.
Jerome's voice (*from the speakers*) Come in, then, come in.
Mervyn's voice (*from the speakers*) How do you do, Mr Watkins. Mervyn Bickerdyke of Child Wellbeing.
Corinna's voice (*from the speakers*) Yes, come on, let's get out of this hideous hall first ...

The screen blanks as they all come inside and the door closes. The sound of them approaching down the hall

> *Corinna enters first, followed closely by Jerome. Mervyn follows behind them. Corinna is, of course, very similar in looks to the original Nan but with little of Nan's submissive nature and a good deal more personal aura, not to mention neuroses. Aged forty, she is formally dressed as though for a business meeting rather than a social event. Mervyn is about the same age. One of those big, gentle, good-natured, pleasant men, he obviously gets by in his job through kindness and tact and by offending no-one—rather than through dynamic personality. At present, he is filled with a nervousness which he can't altogether conceal*

Jerome (*as they enter*) ... I can't help it, there's a fault with the door ...
Corinna There was a fault with the door when I left ...
Jerome Probably because you slammed it so hard when you went, dear.
Mervyn Hallo, Mr Watkins, my name is——

Corinna If I slammed it, I had very just cause.

Jerome (*aware someone is missing*) Where's Geain?

Corinna If anyone had reason to slam a door . . .

Mervyn Mr Watkins, I think I ought to introduce myself—I'm——

Jerome Where the hell's Geain? What have you done with Geain?

Corinna Geain is coming.

Jerome What have you done with her?

Corinna She is coming. Geain is coming.

Jerome When? Because I'm not meeting without her. There's to be no meeting without Geain.

Mervyn Mr Watkins, if I could just nudge my way in a moment to introduce myself——

Corinna Geain went on in the car to buy something. She'll be here in a minute. Anyway, we need to talk without her first.

Jerome You left that child out there in a car on her own . . .?

Corinna Jerome, don't be ridiculous. She is not on her own. It is an armour-plated limousine which cost a fortune to hire—but since that's the only way we could guarantee to get to this place these days . . . She has the driver with her and a man riding—whatever it's called—riding sidegun.

Mervyn Shotgun.

Corinna Shotgun. Thank you, Mr Bickerdyke. Besides which, she is thirteen years old and quite capable of looking after herself.

Mervyn I would endorse that, Mr Watkins.

Jerome (*slightly pacified*) I'm not agreeing anything without Geain having the chance to say what she feels.

Corinna I've no doubt she will. Don't worry.

A slight pause as Corinna inspects the place. Mervyn seizes his chance

Mervyn Look, I'm going to nip right in there for a second, just to say hallo, my name is Merv——

Corinna I must say this place is looking remarkably tidy. You must have been scrubbing at it for weeks.

Jerome Well, we wouldn't want you picking up any nasty germs whilst you were visiting us, would we?

Corinna Us?

Jerome What? (*A great show of having forgotten*) Oh, dear. Oh, heavens. Ah. How could I have forgotten? You haven't met Zoë, have you?

Corinna Zoë?

Jerome Zoë.

Corinna Who or what is Zoë?

Jerome Zoë is my—fiancée.

Corinna Fiancée?

Jerome Yes.

Mervyn Oh. Many congratulations.

Jerome (*to Mervyn*) Thank you very much.

Corinna Did you say fiancée?

Jerome Yes.

Corinna I don't believe it. This is a joke—This is an obscene, grotesque joke. A fiancée . . .?

Jerome Before you meet her, dearest, could I ask you, please—she is very sweet, rather shy—and a little unused to strangers . . . So, please, don't try and be clever with her or embarrass her with awkward questions . . . because she couldn't cope with that. All right? Would that be remotely possible, do you think?

Corinna I don't believe any of this. Not one word.

Jerome (*calling*) Darling!

Nan (*off, from the kitchen*) Hallo, darling?

Corinna My God!

Jerome Darling, what are you doing?

Nan (*off*) I'm just finishing off in here, darling.

Jerome Darling, come on in, they've arrived.

Nan (*off*) Right you are, darling. Just a tick.

Corinna (*rather shaken*) Well, this—certainly does alter things. Doesn't it?

Jerome (*smiling*) Doesn't it?

Nan comes in as before

Nan (*brightly, as she enters*) Hallo! Hallo! Hallo! Welcome! Welcome! Welcome! Sorry. I completely lost track of the time. Typical.

Corinna and Mervyn gape

Jerome Darling, this is Corinna.

Nan Hallo. Corinna. I've heard so much about you.

Corinna (*faintly*) Have you?

Mervyn has never seen anyone quite like her. Jerome is a little easier, now that he is past the first hurdle

Jerome Well, now. I'm sure we'd all like some tea, wouldn't we? Darling, will you fetch the tea, or shall I?

Nan I'll fetch the tea, darling. Excuse me.

Mervyn (*stepping forward to Nan, hand extended*) Hallo, may I just say hallo. My name is——

Nan sweeps past him, unaware. He jumps back

Nan goes out to the kitchen

Corinna Are you telling me that she's living here voluntarily?

Jerome Of course she is. We're engaged.

Corinna Living with *you*?

Jerome Why not?

Corinna But she's—she's——

Mervyn Very much so. Congratulations again.

Corinna Where did you meet her?

Jerome She's an actress.

Mervyn (*impressed*) Really?

Jerome A classical actress.

Corinna Classical?

Nan comes back in unexpectedly. She is empty-handed

Nan (*brightly, as she enters*) Hallo! Hallo! Hallo! Welcome! Welcome! Welcome! Sorry. I——
Jerome (*interrupting swiftly*) Darling, the tea!
Nan (*unflustered*) I'll fetch the tea, darling. Excuse me.

She goes out

A pause

Jerome Excuse me.

He hurries out after Nan to the kitchen

Corinna I think she's wearing one of my old dresses.
Mervyn Oh, yes?
Corinna She's certainly made herself at home here.
Jerome (*off, from the kitchen, shouting fiercely*) Darling, tea! Darling, tea!
Nan (*off, from the kitchen, equally fiercely*) Tea, darling! Tea, darling!

Several loud clangs. The others stare

Jerome hurries back

Jerome Sorry. Just—lending her a hand. Please, sit down.

They sit. Silence. Jerome listens anxiously. He rises. Then sits again

Corinna Does she need any help?
Jerome No, no.

Nan returns. She carries the tea pot and a plate of small cakes

Nan (*to the seated assembly*) Do sit down, everyone.
Mervyn (*rising, apologetically*) Sorry, I . . .
Nan Nice pot of tea.
Jerome Oh, super. Clever little cuddles.
Nan And some home-made cakes.
Jerome (*rather over-enthusiastically*) Home-made cakes! Wonderful! Wonderful! Yummy, yummy, yum-yum.
Mervyn You made these yourself?
Jerome Yes, she did. Didn't you, darling, you made these yourself?
Nan I made them myself, darling. (*She grabs the tea pot rather jerkily*) Tea, everyone?
Jerome (*hastily taking the tea pot from her*) I'll pour the tea. (*As he pours*) You relax. You've been at it all day. Precious.

Nan rises at once and kisses him on the cheek

(*Rather coyly*) Oh, come on. Not in front of everyone . . .

He laughs. Nan laughs in response. Corinna stares in disbelief

Corinna I think I'm going to be sick.

Jerome (*to the others*) She's been at it all day. Slaving away in that kitchen. Then she was up at dawn, scouring the place from top to bottom. She never stops. All day. Now, do we want milk or lemon? (*To Nan*) Darling, you won't have anything, I take it.

Nan I won't have anything, I take it, darling.

Jerome (*to the others*) Eats nothing at all. Fierce diet.

Corinna (*rather sourly*) Doesn't look as if she needs to bother.

Jerome She doesn't. Wonderful metabolism. Milk?

Corinna Lemon.

Mervyn I'll have milk, thank you.

Jerome finishes serving the tea, helping himself as he does so

Could I stick a foot in the door here just to take this opportunity to say hallo, formally? I'm Mervyn Bickerdyke, Child Wellbeing, of course. I spoke to you on the phone, Mr Watkins. Eventually.

Jerome Yes, so you did. Sandwich?

Mervyn Thank you. (*Smiling at Nan*) Seeing as they were made with your own fair hands.

Nan ignores him. Corinna grabs a sandwich, irritably

I'm sorry. After you, after you.

All, except Nan, help themselves to sandwiches

We were just hearing, Zoë, that you were an actress.

Corinna Classical, is that right?

Jerome That's right, isn't it? You're a classical actress, aren't you, little blossom?

Nan Oh yes. Arkadina in Chekhov and Queen Margaret in *See How They Run*.

Corinna (*puzzled*) Really?

Jerome That was the—Royal Shakespeare production, of course——

Mervyn Of course. Now, to the reason we've all met——

Something starts to bleep somewhere about his person. Jerome checks Nan nervously

—we've ... Oh. Would you excuse me. My bleeper. (*He rises*)

Jerome (*waving towards the console*) Do you want to make a——?

Mervyn No, no. I have my portable here. Thank you very much.

Mervyn moves away from them to a far corner of the room. He produces a wafer-thin pocket phone from his jacket and answers his call. He stops bleeping. He murmurs indistinctly while the others continue their tea

Corinna Well, I have to confess, Jerome, that I am simply amazed. I didn't think anyone could do it, Zoë. Make a civilized animal out of this man.

She laughs. Nan laughs in response

Jerome I'm putty in her hands, darling, aren't I, precious?

Nan Aren't you, precious?

She gets up and kisses him on the cheek and sits again. Corinna glares at them, disgusted by this blissful scene

Corinna Don't think I don't know why you're doing this, both of you. Trying to impress that—(*indicating Mervyn*)—limp lettuce over there ... God, he's wet. Three hours we were in that car with him bleating away. That's when his bleeper wasn't going. He was either bleeping or bleating, like a radio-controlled sheep. God, I despair of men these days, I despair. They're all so lank. And dank.

Jerome (*to Nan*) My ex-wife airing her views in general.

Corinna Well, ask Zoë. I bet you she feels the same. Zoë, outside this very special little love-nest, this haven of domestic fervour, don't you find most men these days utterly spineless and flaccid? I mean, that's just talking to them—I'm not even talking about bed. Don't you agree, Zoë?

Nan looks blank

Yes, she does. She's just being loyal, poor thing.

Jerome She knows when to keep quiet, don't you, Zoë?

Corinna She'd need to. Living with you.

She laughs. Nan, responding to this, laughs too. Corinna looks at her rather sharply, sizing up her rival afresh

Yes, you're a deep one, aren't you, Zoë? Quite a lot going on in there, I imagine.

Jerome You bet.

Mervyn finishes the call and rejoins them

Mervyn Sorry. Never far away from the office when you've got one of those. (*He waves his phone*)

Corinna I thought you said you had two of them?

Mervyn Ah, yes. I have my private home phone as well. In case my wife wants to get hold of me.

Corinna (*sweetly*) But that one doesn't ring very often, I imagine?

Mervyn (*missing that*) Right. Where were we? Yes. Young Geain——

Jerome Look, if we're going to start talking, I think Zoë would rather—get on with other things.

Corinna Oh, surely not?

Jerome Well, she was saying earlier she felt she'd feel a bit in the way. And she does have some work to get on with. Darling, if you want to go and study now ...

Nan (*rising at once*) I want to go and study now, darling.

She goes out to the bedrooms

Corinna No, no, this is ridiculous, she must stay. Zoë! (*To Jerome*) Jerome, tell her to come back at once, for heaven's sake, she needs to hear all this.

Jerome No, she really does need to do some work. She has a big audition tomorrow.

Mervyn Really? What's that for?

Jerome For a musical.
Mervyn (*more impressed still*) Does she sing as well?
Jerome Like an angel.
Corinna How else? None the less, if she really is intending to live here with you, possibly even marry you—God help her—she ought to be in on the discussions . . .
Mervyn It would be advisable.
Jerome (*reluctantly*) Well. For a few minutes. (*Calling*) Darling!
Nan (*off*) Hallo, darling!
Jerome (*calling*) Darling, come back.
Nan (*off*) Right you are, darling, just a tick.
Jerome She's coming.
Mervyn (*indicating the sandwiches*) May I . . .?
Jerome waves for him to go ahead. Mervyn evidently enjoys his food

Corinna Has she hurt her leg?
Jerome What?
Corinna She appears to be limping.
Jerome Oh, she damaged it—while she was rushing around dancing.
Mervyn She dances as well?
Jerome No-one to touch her . . .
Corinna I'm longing to see her fly.

Nan enters

Nan (*brightly, as she enters*) Hallo! Hallo! Hallo! Welc——
Jerome (*cutting her off*) Darling, we want you to sit here with us.
Nan (*sitting*) Yes, darling.
Mervyn Maybe we can persuade you to sing for us before we leave, Zoë.
Jerome I'm afraid not.
Mervyn No?
Jerome No. She's saving the voice.
Mervyn Oh, I see.
Jerome Professionals. They have to be very careful how often they sing.
Corinna Or even speak, apparently. (*She smiles at Nan*)
Mervyn Well. I think we ought to—make a start, then. The question we have to decide first, regarding Geain, is whether—— (*He starts to beep again*) I'm sorry. Please excuse me——
Corinna (*exasperated*) Oh, dear God.
Mervyn Don't worry, I'll put them on to answer. It's the office again, I'll put them on to answer. (*He fumbles in another pocket as he continues to beep*)
Jerome (*intrigued*) You have an answering machine on you as well?
Corinna If you turn him upside down, he also makes ice-cream.
Mervyn (*rather proudly*) I've got a few wires about my person, yes, I have to admit it. (*He finds his answering machine and switches it on. The beeping stops. Producing items from various pockets and holding them up to show them*) Answering machine. Neat, eh? Home phone. Office phone. Oh, this is an interesting one. Location finder. If you're ever hopelessly lost. Switch it on and it can pinpoint your on-ground position to within twelve

square metres. French. Of course. Then you've got this—excuse me. (*He takes off his jacket to reveal that the whole of his neck and arms are encased in a criss-cross of wires*) This is a personal alarm system. Latest type. West German. Naturally. Made by Heisser-Hausen Zeiplussen. They're a subsidiary of Glotz.

Jerome (*vaguely*) Oh, yes.

Mervyn Any physical attack on my person and this thing screams the place down.

Corinna Do you need a machine to do it for you?

Mervyn (*putting on his jacket again*) Ah, but what if I was rendered unconscious? I couldn't scream at all, could I? Whereas this thing. Two kilometre radius—up to an hour, guaranteed. And it automatically phones the police.

Corinna And you certainly couldn't do that if you were unconscious, could you? Must take you ages getting dressed in the morning.

Mervyn Maybe. But I can get undressed quick enough, if called upon to do so, don't you worry about that.

He laughs at his own roguish wit. Corinna looks at him coldly. Nan responds, laughing

(*Winking at Nan as he sits again*) Sorry. Mustn't get me on to these things. Fatal. My hobby, rather.

Jerome Have some more to eat.

Mervyn Thank you. (*He helps himself*)

Corinna Lovely home-made cakes, Zoë. Clever you. Very, very like those new deep-frozen ones you bake in the packet. But yours are twice as good. (*She smiles at Nan again*)

Mervyn Getting back to Geain, then. We mustn't get sidetracked, must we? We——

The phone rings in the room

Ignore it. Ignore that. I'm on answer, ignore it.

Jerome That's my phone.

Mervyn Oh, is it? Yes, of course, that's your phone . . .

He laughs. Nan laughs as well

Corinna That woman laughs at anything.

Jerome She's got a sense of humour. That's why I love her. Don't I, precious?

Nan kisses him

Corinna Oh, do stop it, both of you.

The answering machine picks up the incoming call. On screen, Lupus appears. He is still in the club phone box but there seems to be some sort of riot going on round him. There also appears to be something on fire, judging from the smoke and the flames reflected on his face. He looks somewhat the worse for wear

My God, it's not him . . .

Lupus Hi, Jerry, mate. I'll have to make this a quick one. Lupus, still at the old Cockatoo. I hope the answering machine doesn't mean you're on your way here. Anyway, this is to say, if you do get this message, don't bother coming down. It's got a bit rough here ...

Jerome gets up and crosses to the console

Jerome Excuse me.

Lupus Apparently, this afternoon the club was booked by two hundred members of the Motorhead Nostalgic Appreciation Society. I ask you, Jerry—Motorhead! Where have they been? I said to one of them, listen, if it's nostalgia you're into then do yourself a favour, treat yourself to the Moody Blues and listen to real music. I mean, really——

His voice is cut off as Jerome fades him down

Corinna Good old Lupus.

Mervyn Do you need to make any calls on his behalf? His lawyer or something? It looked quite serious ...

Jerome No, no. He's all right. That's always happening to Lupus. Nothing out of the ordinary.

On screen, the phone booth topples on to its side. Lupus goes with it, still gesticulating and talking. None of them notices this. The screen goes blank

There you are, you see, he's hung up.

Corinna The man is a walking state of emergency. Is he still with that woman? With Deborah?

Nan makes a little strangled sound

Or is she off with somebody else's husband again?

Jerome I really wouldn't know. Look, let's——

Corinna Dear little Deborah, I wonder how she is these days?

Nan reacts again and does so every time Deborah's name is mentioned

Heard anything from Deborah lately, have you, Zoë?

Jerome I don't think Zoë wants to talk about Deborah and nor do I.

Corinna I'm sure you don't. But how do you know Zoë doesn't?

Jerome Because she doesn't.

Corinna Have you asked her? Ask her.

Mervyn (*jocularly*) I think I'd quite like to hear about Deborah from the sound of things ...

He laughs. Nan laughs. Jerome glares at him

Corinna Go on. Ask her.

Jerome There isn't the faintest chance is there, darling, you want to hear about Deborah?

Nan I want to hear about Deborah, darling.

Corinna (*scenting blood*) There you are. I told you she did. Of course she does. Everyone should know about Deborah, shouldn't they? The Deborahs of this world need discussing. They need a constant airing—in her

case, literally. Zoë needs to know. Forewarned is forearmed. And I'm
sure Mr Bickerdyke here, who can get undressed very, very quickly if
called upon to do so, might like to be warned about Deborah, too.

Jerome Look, come on, Corinna, why drag that up again ...

Mervyn I think we might be in essence be straying away from the basic
issues here ... (*He beeps again*) Ignore that. Ignore that! That is me, this
time, that is definitely me.

Corinna (*confidentially, to Nan*) Never mind, Zoë. Later, when we're alone,
darling, I'll tell you all about Deborah. (*She laughs*)

Nan (*laughing*) You'll tell me all about Deborah, darling.

Corinna I think Zoë and I have a lot more in common than I thought.

Jerome I don't think Zoë has anything to say to you at all.

Corinna What's the matter? Frightened she might hear the truth?

Jerome Not at all.

Corinna That's a man's greatest nightmare, isn't it? All the women in his life
getting together and talking about him. What's he like at breakfast,
darling? What's he like in bed?

Nan He'll soon get the hang of it again, I'm sure.

Corinna blinks

Corinna What did she say?

Jerome laughs loudly. Nan follows suit

Jerome God, this girl's sense of humour is wicked sometimes. Wicked. Isn't
it, precious?

Nan kisses him. Corinna is very puzzled

Corinna (*staring at them both*) Yes ...

Mervyn I think if I could hop, step and jump in again at this point. Just—
looking at the time ...

Corinna Listen, we can keep this very simple. The situation is this. Geain
has reached an age now when I am more than happy for us both to share
responsibility, Jerome. I am happy that she sees you. I am happy that she
spends time with you.

Jerome You what?

Corinna My only——

Jerome You are saying this now, after ...?

Corinna My only——

Jerome After four years of ...?

Corinna May I please finish? My only misgiving has been the thought of
Geain coming to see you here. The combination of you, the flat and the
general state of this neighbourhood always seemed to me strong enough
reason to prevent her coming. Well, the neighbourhood certainly hasn't
improved but—thanks I suspect to Zoë, quite a lot else has. So I withdraw
my objections. Geain may come and see you if she likes, whenever she
likes.

Jerome Do you hear that, Mr Bickerdyke?

Mervyn Yes, indeed.

Jerome You are bearing witness to this?
Mervyn I am.
Jerome Well. That's that, isn't it?
Corinna Presumably. It's up to Geain. That's if Mr Bickerdyke has no
objections?
Jerome You don't have objections?
Mervyn No, no ...
Jerome There's no problem, is there?
Mervyn Well ...
Jerome What?
Mervyn There is one aspect with which I'm not entirely happy, I have to
confess. I mean, although the youngster has to come first, indeed her
interests are of paramount importance—everyone, in a sense, needs to be
considered. And I'm not altogether convinced that there aren't certain
individuals—certain aspects of the existing—(*he beeps; in time, he goes on
to "answer"*)—ignore that—please—ignore that—aspects of the existing
status quo that could suffer—as the result of any subsequent modified
arrangements—regarding the possible—alteration of the present—custo-
dianship of the youngster. As of this present time.

Corinna makes a loud snoring noise

If you follow me.
Jerome Do I take it you are not happy for Geain to come here?
Mervyn Well ...
Jerome You don't consider us suitable?
Mervyn It's difficult to put into words ...
Jerome I'm her father.
Mervyn Oh, quite.
Jerome And Zoë loves children. She adores them. She was saying so only
the other day. Tell them your feelings towards children.

A slight pause. Nan does not react

(*Remembering the key word*) Sweetheart.
Nan (*promptly*) I'd love to have children of my own. Wouldn't it be lovely
to hear them rushing about the flat, laughing and yelling? With the right
man—someone who'd share them—they'd be everything I ever wanted. I
suppose you're either maternal or you aren't. I know which I am.

A silence

Jerome (*moved*) Darling, thank you.
Nan Thank you, darling.
Mervyn (*rather moved*) Well, what can one say ...?
Corinna What indeed?
Mervyn I'll be honest with you, Mr Watkins. What I've experienced here
this afternoon has been for me—as a married man myself—heart-
warming. You and your—fiancée—Zoë—well—you can feel it when you
walk in the door. You can almost sense the happiness.
Jerome There you are, then.

Mervyn It's just that I'm a little afraid of what might happen if we introduced
Geain into this house. There is, on the one hand, the real hope that your
own happiness could have a beneficial effect on the youngster——
Jerome It's bound to.
Mervyn Ah, but it has been known to happen, that because the couple were
so contented, the introduction of the youngster actually upset the happy
status quo. And the couple became unhappy as a result of having the
youngster with them. Consequently, the youngster was no longer in
a happy home but an unhappy one. Which naturally in turn made it,
the youngster, feel guilty because it felt responsible for causing that
unhappiness. Which had the knock-on effect, of course, of making the
youngster unhappy, which won't do at all. Because, after all, the bottom
line is the happiness of the youngster, is it or is it not, correct me if I'm
wrong?

A pause. They stare at him, trying to work out what he's said

Corinna Your job's a good deal more complicated than most people
imagine, isn't it, Mr Bickerdyke?
Jerome You feel that Geain might upset me and Zoë?
Mervyn I'm saying she could. At her present stage of adolescence. Which
is—complex.
Jerome And that, in turn, would upset Geain?
Mervyn It's possible.
Jerome Well, that's simple enough. If that happens I'll get rid of her.
Mervyn I beg your pardon?
Jerome I'll get rid of her.
Mervyn Get rid of Geain?
Jerome No, of course not. Not Geain. I'll get rid of Zoë. That's easy
enough.
Mervyn (*stunned*) You'd get rid of her?
Jerome Yes. We'd—you know—split up. For the sake of the child.
Mervyn Just like that?
Corinna What does Zoë have to say about that?
Jerome Darling, you wouldn't mind us splitting up for the sake of the child?
Nan I wouldn't mind us splitting up for the sake of the child, darling.
Jerome There you are, you see, she doesn't mind at all.
Mervyn But that's what you did before.
Jerome What?
Mervyn You and your wife. That's what you did before. That's the root of
the problem now. You can't do that again. Think of the youngster. We
must think of the youngster, Mr Watkins.
Jerome Yes, that was with her mother. That was different. I mean, this is
only with—only—with . . .

A pause

Corinna Only some woman or other, he was going to say.
Jerome No.
Corinna Well, Zoë. You're taking this all very calmly, dear. I hope you

know what you're doing. Personally, I'd have punched your precious fiancé on the nose.

Nan kisses Jerome on the cheek

Oh well, save your breath. Never mind, Zoë, if you're very good in this life, you might just come back in the next as a shoe-cleaning kit. You'll enjoy that.

Jerome There is no need to be offensive, Corinna. Just because the sight of two people completely and hopelessly in love distresses you, there's——

Corinna In love? Jerome, you are treating this woman like a doormat. How dare you? And Zoë, for heaven's sake, darling, stand up for yourself.

Nan stands up

Nan (*swiftly*) Standing up, darling.
Jerome (*swiftly*) Darling, sit down.
Nan (*sitting*) Sitting down, darling.
Mervyn Listen, I must just be allowed to finish the point I started making ... Which is, that this is all a big hypothetical if. Much more likely is that Geain will respond to the peaceful friendly ambience and the reverse will happen. The relationship between the three of you will take root and blossom ...
Nan Oh, yes. Arkadina in Chekhov and Queen Margaret in *See How They Run.*
Mervyn I beg your pardon?
Corinna What?
Jerome She wants to go and study. Darling, you need to go and study.
Nan (*rising immediately*) I need to go and study, darling.

Nan goes off to the bedrooms

Mervyn Do you think you may have offended her?
Corinna Impossible.
Mervyn I don't know, some people may not care to be referred to as shoe-cleaning equipment.
Corinna Oh, surely not in Zoë's case? Living with Jerome, that comes under the heading of a compliment.

Mervyn looks at his watch

Mervyn They're rather late, aren't they? I think I might phone the car. Do you think that would be an idea? Make sure they're all right?
Corinna If you like.
Jerome Do you want to use the ...? (*He indicates his phone*)
Mervyn No, no. I'll use my other line. It's quite all right.

He moves off to the hall to speak in private

Corinna Well. Congratulations, Jerome. I'm very, very, very pleased for you. I'm delighted. (*Pause*) I'm so thrilled, you've no idea. (*Pause*) No, really, I am. I'm being perfectly sincere. (*Pause*) At least one of us has managed to ... (*Pause*) I'm really pleased. Honestly. You must be—so happy. (*Pause*) You're very lucky, both of you. (*Pause*) She's lovely and obviously wonderful for you and you're both very much in love. (*Pause*) Who could ask for anything more?

Jerome I couldn't. (*He smiles*)

Corinna No.

A pause

(*With sudden suppressed fury*) You smug bastard.

Mervyn returns from the hall

Mervyn Sorry to interrupt . . . They're here. The car's just arrived. Apparently, they were——

He is cut short by the doorbell ringing. The face of a short-haired, dark-chinned hermaphrodite appears on the screen

Mervyn Ah, I'll get it. I'll get it.

He goes out to the hall again

Jerome No, don't open the door without . . . (*Seeing what is on the screen*) No, don't open it. Don't let that thing in here.

On screen, Mervyn opens the door

What's he doing? (*Diving for his swordstick*) What's that idiot think he's doing? He's letting in every monster in the neighbourhood.

Corinna Jerome, dear. That is Geain.

Jerome What?

Geain enters the flat and closes the door. The screen blanks

Corinna That's your daughter. That's Geain. Remember?

Jerome (*stunned*) Geain? That is Geain?

Geain enters. In the flesh, she looks if anything slightly more grotesque. She wears a not unfamiliar parody of male work clothes circa 1955. But hers are carried to some extreme. Heavy boots, cord trousers with a wide leather belt, padded rather incongruously at the crotch, old, faded shirt open at the neck to reveal the currently fashionable "hairy vest", i.e. an undershirt knotted with a mass of supposed chest hair. The back of her jacket is studded with the words: SONS OF BITCHES. Her hair is short, brushed straight back and oiled; her only make-up the blue-chinned, unshaven look

Geain (*cursorily*) 'Llo.

She strides into the room, picks up a sandwich and sits, without ceremony or introduction. Her brusqueness, one suspects, also hides a shyness. Jerome stares, thunderstruck. He retains the swordstick throughout the next

Corinna Here she is.

Geain (*scowling*) He.

Corinna Sorry, my mistake. He. You remember your—son Geain, don't you? This is your father, dear.

Geain (*nodding to Jerome*) 'Llo.

Jerome manages to open and shut his mouth. Geain crams another sandwich into her mouth

Mervyn (*with inappropriate avuncularity*) Did you manage to buy that game you were looking for, Geain?
Geain (*scowling*) No.
Mervyn Oh, why was that?
Geain (*muttering*) Daughters.
Mervyn What's that?
Geain Daughters.
Mervyn Tortoise?
Geain Daughters. Daughters of Darkness.
Mervyn Oh, those, yes. What about them?
Geain Wouldn't let me in.
Mervyn Wouldn't let you in? In where? In the shop?
Geain No.
Mervyn Why ever not?
Geain They hate us. We hate them.
Mervyn Oh, dear. That's not very friendly, is it?
Corinna They're great rivals apparently. Amazing as it may sound, the Sons of Bitches and the Daughters of Darkness aren't speaking to each other at all.
Geain Rancid sows.
Corinna (*to Jerome*) Your son, you will observe, has joined the Male Dominance Movement—the Top Missionaries ... whatever they're called.
Geain (*through her sandwich*) The Missionary Position.
Corinna Missionary Position.

A silence

Well, I've no doubt you two will have lots to talk about. (*Pause*) Talking of missionaries, shouldn't you call Zoë? She should meet Geain, surely?
Mervyn Oh, yes. Let's bring Zoë in.
Jerome (*still dazed, calling*) Darling!
Nan (*off, from the bedroom*) Hallo, darling?
Jerome Darling, come in. My—my—Geain's arrived.
Nan (*off*) Right you are, darling. Just a tick.
Corinna Zoë is Dad's new friend, Geain. His fiancée.

Geain looks at Jerome scornfully. Jerome looks at Geain and gives a little despairing moan

Geain Huh!

Nan enters from the bedroom

Nan (*brightly, as she enters*) Hallo! Hallo! Hallo! Welcome! Welcome! Welcome! Sorry. I completely lost tra——
Corinna This is Geain, Zoë. Geain, say hallo to Zoë.

Geain stares at Nan. Nan stares at Geain. For various reasons, neither of them speaks

Ah. (*Softly*) Geain, at least say hallo.
Geain 'Llo.
Jerome (*rather automatically*) Darling. This is Geain. Treasure.
Nan (*at once*) Well, who's this beautiful little girl, then? You must be Geain, mustn't you? Well, Geain, I'm Zoë. And we're going to be very, very good friends, aren't we? I hope we are. Now would you like to come into the kitchen with me and I'll give you a big glass of orange, how about that? Come on, then, come with Zoë . . .
Geain (*backing away from Nan's outstretched hand*) Get off. Get her off me.
Nan Off we go. I've got a big surprise for you out here, Geain.

Before anyone can stop them, Nan has dragged the protesting Geain off to the kitchen

Corinna (*somewhat alarmed*) Geain won't drink orange juice, Jerome . . .
Jerome Hang on, I'll stop her, I'll . . . (*He makes to follow them*)
Mervyn (*quite forcefully, for him*) No, no, no, no, no.

Jerome stops

Jerome What?
Mervyn Leave them together. Please. The very best thing that can happen. A chance for them to get to know each other.
Jerome Yes, but—she wasn't supposed to do all that—she——
Mervyn Please. Trust my judgement. I am trained in these matters.
Corinna She'll never get Geain to drink orange juice, I can tell you that.
Mervyn Then they will no doubt resolve matters between them. Geain will tell Zoë no, thank you, Zoë, I do not want orange juice, thank you very much indeed, I would like a glass of milk. Or somesuch.
Corinna Or somesuch.
Mervyn And Zoë will no doubt defer to Geain's request and give her what she wants.
Jerome Possibly.
Mervyn And that way a bond will be formed between them. We call that, in my line of work, a Self-Seeding Relationship.

There is a crash from the kitchen

Nan (*off*) Oh, for goodness' sake, you extremely stupid old bat. Who put that there, then?

Jerome makes to go off again

Jerome I'd better just go and——
Mervyn No, no, no. Please, please, Mr Watkins. Trust me.
Jerome It's just, you see, that Zoë isn't——
Mervyn No, I appreciate that. Zoë is not used to youngsters and she'll have to learn as she goes. No doubt she'll make mistakes. Being human, it would be extraordinary if she didn't.
Jerome It would.

Mervyn But what's happening out there is a mutual exploration process. Now, please. Leave them to explore each other. Let's all sit down, keep calm and allow nature to take its course.

They sit. A silence. A crash

Corinna Jerome, she'll kill her. If you leave them together, she'll kill her.

Mervyn Ah-ah-ah-ah-ah-ah-ah ...

Corinna Well, we could at least listen to them, couldn't we? See they're all right? I take it the rooms are still wired for sound? Did you know, Mr Bickerdyke, he records everything? Be careful. When Geain and I lived here—every word, every breath we took was recorded and played back to us.

Jerome Nonsense.

Corinna It's true.

Jerome I never played half of it back to you.

Mervyn (*who has been listening more towards the kitchen*) They seem very quiet now. I'm sure things are going to be fine. We mustn't expect results straightaway but—it's a start.

Corinna I still don't think she should be left out there alone with her ...

Jerome I don't know. Maybe it's all right. Zoë's—very gentle ...

Corinna I'm talking about Geain. Nobody tells Geain what to drink. I've still got this bruise where she kicked me because I bought the wrong biscuits.

Jerome I hope she doesn't try and kick Zoë.

Corinna Yes, she's turned into a right little thug, your daughter. First suggestion she isn't going to get her own way, she punches and kicks. Good luck. That's all I can say. Maybe you'll have more success with your child than I have ...

Another crash from the kitchen

Jerome Let me get one thing clear. That—thing in there is no relation of mine—that transvestite truck driver ...

Mervyn Mr Watkins——

Jerome (*with a cry*) What have you done with my little girl? I want my little girl. I've never seen that thing before. (*Yelling at Corinna*) What is it? I don't want that. (*Advancing on her, brandishing the swordstick*) Take it away! Screw it back on the church roof where it belongs ...

Mervyn (*wresting the swordstick from him*) Mr Watkins, will you please control yourself?

The two men stand panting. Mervyn now has the swordstick

Corinna It's all right, Mr Bickerdyke, I'm accustomed to these outbursts, believe me. In reply to your question, Jerome, I have done nothing— because there was nothing that I or anyone else could do. Geain does what Geain likes and stuff the rest of the world. I can't think who she— sorry he—inherits that particularly unpleasant side of his nature from, so we can only hazard a guess. But he—she—it does what it likes. It goes to school, it has friends, it wants to be like its friends. If its friends choose to dress up like that, I can't stop it. Because, as it explains to me, if it doesn't dress up like its friends then it won't have any friends any more. I have to admit that it's not a great deal of fun having a female male chauvinist kicking me all day, demanding to be waited on hand and foot and referring to me as a dozy cow. But looking at some of the alternatives it might have chosen, I've decided to grin and bear it. Now if you want to try and alter her, you're welcome to try. Go ahead. Please. Because I really do need help, Jerome. I can't do it alone. I really believed, after I left you, that I could cope with anything. I was wrong. I cannot cope with Geain as she is now. Maybe in a few years, when she's . . . There you are, I admit it. And I am shocked by my own inadequacy. I am even a little ashamed. It's made a trifle more bearable because I'm absolutely certain that nobody else, in these circumstances, could have coped any better than I did.

Mervyn (*gently*) I'm sure you've done everything that a single parent could, Corinna.

A brief silence

It's very quiet out there, isn't it?

Before they can move, Nan comes back from the kitchen. She waits by the doorway

Nan Here she is, Mummy. Here she is, Daddy.

Geain comes in slowly from the kitchen. She looks slightly dazed. Her face is now clean, almost gleaming. She has on a too-long nightdress. She carries a large frilly doll in her arms

Jerome (*muttering*) Oh, my God . . .
Corinna (*stunned*) Geain!
Mervyn Well . . .
Nan And what are we going to sing, Geain?

Geain scowls

Geain. (*Prompting her*) "Baa baa . . ."
Geain I'm not saying that . . .
Nan All together.
  Baa baa black sheep, whither do you wander?
  Four and twenty blackbirds baked on a tuffet—good—
  The little dog laughed to see such fun
  And said what a good boy am I. Woof! Moo! Well done.

Nan claps. The others follow suit in a perplexed manner

Geain (*not without admiration*) She's mad.
Mervyn That's a new one on me, certainly. (*He laughs*)
Nan (*laughing, taking hold of Geain's hand*) Now we're off to bed. Good-night, everyone. Say good-night.
Geain I'm not saying good-night.
Nan (*dragging her away*) That's it.

Geain (*struggling vainly as they go*) I can't go to bed now, you dumb woman . . .

They go off to the bedrooms. A cry from Geain

Nan (*off*) Oh, for goodness' sake, you extremely stupid old bat. Who put that there, then?

They stare at each other

Mervyn Well, I must say. In all my years, I've . . . What a remarkable woman. Quite remarkable.

Jerome is aware that Corinna is quite upset

Jerome Well, it's—it's just part of her—basic—original—I mean it was there already in her, you see . . .

Mervyn As it is within all women, Mr Watkins. All women. (*A pause*) Well, that's a problem solved.

Corinna Would you think it terribly rude of me, Mr Bickerdyke, if I were to ask you to leave us alone for a moment?

Mervyn Ah, well . . .

Corinna Actually, I don't really care if you do find it terribly rude of me. Would you go, anyway.

Mervyn (*springing up*) Yes, of course. I'll—I'll wait in the . . . (*He indicates the kitchen*)

Jerome The kitchen.

Mervyn I'll wait in there, shall I? I have to phone my . . . Yes. Excuse me. (*He puts down the swordstick and takes a handful of sandwiches as he goes*) Excuse me. (*After a glance at them both, he picks up the swordstick again*)

Mervyn goes to the kitchen

Corinna and Jerome are silent for a second

Corinna All I want to say is—I think I'll leave now. Quietly. I'll leave Geain with you and Zoë. All right?

Jerome Ah.

Corinna Well, that's what you'd like, isn't it? That's what you wanted?

Jerome Yes.

Corinna I mean obviously she'll have to return to me—at some point—she has to go back to school for one thing. But she could stay here for a couple of weeks, anyway. See how it works out.

Jerome You're happy to do that? You think that's best?

Corinna Frankly, Jerome, I feel so demoralized I don't know what I think. All I actually feel like doing is crying. I mean, that woman's done more with that kid in five minutes than I managed in five years.

Jerome That's just her being a stranger, she——

Corinna I might have been able to cope with that, if Zoë'd at least been— terribly plain or—homely—or . . . I thought for one glorious moment she was actually very dim. But then, of course, it turns out she isn't. She's obviously very intelligent, shrewd, cool, sexy, wonderful with kids, a great actress, singer, dancer, terrific in bed—the only thing she lies about are her cakes—and it's bloody unfair, Jerome. (*She starts to cry*)

Jerome Oh now, come on——

Corinna How can it be allowed to happen? After all you've done? All the
rotten, traitorous, lousy, underhand things you've done to me. What right
have you to somebody like that? You're a bastard, Jerome. You're barely
human. What have you ever done in your life to deserve *anyone*?

Jerome Well, I can't answer that . . . I really can't.

Corinna There is no justice. That's all. None. Here's me . . . (*She sniffs*) I
haven't found anyone, do you know that? Nobody.

Jerome Ah, that's only because you have very high standards. Quite
rightly . . .

Corinna I've got no standards at all. Not any more. I'll take anyone who's
available. I'm a forty-year-old bank manager who sits crying in her office.
What use is that to anybody? Do you know I gave a man a loan the other
day solely on the grounds that I wanted to go to bed with him?

Jerome My God. And did you?

Corinna Of course I didn't. I found out he only borrowed the money so he
could get married. I'm losing my judgement, I'm losing my confidence
and then that bloody child comes home from school and kicks me because
of a packet of biscuits. I can't cope any more. I just want to go somewhere
and lie down.

Jerome stares at her, amazed

(*Amused, despite herself, by his expression*) There! I bet you never thought
you'd hear me talking like this. (*Pause*) How did she get Geain to *wash*? I
never got her to wash. She stank to high heaven. Sweat is macho. Well.
Tell Zoë to keep up the good work. I'll collect the exciting Mr Bickerdyke
and slink away.

Jerome Yes. Well, you never know your luck, you may——

Corinna Don't you dare. Don't even suggest it. I have a fragment of pride
left. Well, cheer up. You're not allowed to be miserable. You've got what
you wanted, haven't you?

Jerome Yes.

Corinna As you usually do. (*Pause*) I'll tell you something amusing, shall I?
You know, half the reason I came here was to see how you felt about—
felt about, you know, coming back.

Jerome Coming back?

Corinna Yes, I—well, when I thought you were still on your own here, I
thought that we might all three get together. Have another go. But I
didn't know about Zoë, of course. Now she's staked her claim, I don't
think I could compete with that. Not the state I'm in at present. (*Pause*)
Still, I thought that would amuse you.

Pause. She rises

Jerome (*slowly*) Just a second . . .

Corinna I'll call Mr Bickerdyke.

Jerome Wait . . .

Corinna I don't think there's much else to say, Jerome.

Jerome There's something I need to tell you. Please.

Corinna No, I don't want to hear about——

Jerome No, you see, things are not—altogether as they seem. The reason Zoë is here at all is because—I needed someone here—to impress you.

Corinna Well, she did, well done.

Jerome No, that's the only reason she's here, you see, so that you and Mr Bickerdyke—so you'd let Geain stay here. Because it looked OK.

Corinna What exactly are you saying? Are you saying that Zoë is only here for our benefit?

Jerome Yes.

Corinna She isn't here normally?

Jerome No.

Corinna Then who is she?

Jerome She's—she's an actress. She really is an actress. This is just a—short engagement. So to speak.

Corinna What did you do, hire her?

Jerome Right.

Corinna (*staring at him*) I see. I see. (*She is exercising a great effort of self-control*)

Jerome (*watching her, apprehensively*) So that's OK, then, isn't it? I mean, now you don't have to be upset. Do you? You don't need to feel jealous of Zoë. Or—or inadequate. Or unattractive. She's just an actress—who—who looks good and can handle children. But she's nothing compared with you. I mean, if you'd only said you—you wanted us to—Well, that's great. You know, that's what I wanted? Isn't that amazing? That's exactly what I wanted. There we were, the two of us—both wanting the same thing—and ... Isn't life sometimes little short of miraculous? (*Pause*) Alleluiah!

Corinna (*icily*) I hope you're recording all of this, Jerome. You'll no doubt have such a good laugh playing it back to yourself later. (*Calling*) Mr Bickerdyke.

Jerome What the hell's the matter, now?

Corinna Mr Bickerdyke!

Mervyn returns from the kitchen. He is putting away his phone

Mervyn Coming. Just talking to the wife. We're having a dinner party tonight. My big chief is coming. With her husband. My wife reckons my chief is after me for bigger things. I said to my wife, I don't care what she's after so long as it isn't my body. (*He laughs*)

Corinna (*frostily*) We're just leaving, Mr Bickerdyke.

Mervyn When you're ready. All settled?

Jerome Leaving? I thought——

Corinna I'll just fetch Geain. She must get dressed. (*Calling as she goes*) Geain!

Mervyn Geain! But I thought ...

Corinna goes off towards the bedrooms

What's happening? I thought Geain was staying.

Jerome Yes. Things seem to have . . . changed. Something seems to have caused Corinna to change her mind.

Mervyn Yes? Well—strictly between us, Mr Watkins—your ex-wife appears to me to be a woman operating under some considerable inner stress.

Jerome Yes?

Mervyn Not, if you'll pardon my humour, quite the woman you'd want to see handling your investments. (*He laughs*)

Corinna returns

Corinna Right. I've called her.

Mervyn What's caused the change of plan, may I inquire?

Corinna I'm afraid, Mr Bickerdyke, we've both been the victim of one of my husband's practical jokes.

Mervyn We have?

Corinna Zoë is not what she appears. She was merely rented by Jerome for the afternoon. She doesn't belong here and she doesn't live here.

Mervyn But why . . .? (*To Jerome*) Why did you do that?

Corinna To deceive you, Mr Bickerdyke, and to make a fool of me. That's why.

Jerome That is not why I did it——

Corinna (*calling*) Geain! If we leave now, Jerome, you can send your actress home early. You may even get some of your money back. I presume she's rented by the hour.

Jerome I don't understand you. I thought you'd be pleased.

Corinna Delighted. Thank you so much.

Mervyn I don't follow this, I don't follow this at all.

Geain appears, still in her "nightdress", holding Nan's hand. They stop in the doorway

Corinna Come along, Geain, there's been a slight confusion, we're going home.

Jerome Just a second, just a second . . .

Mervyn Now, let me get this straight. Are we saying that this woman—that Zoë is not living here with you? She is not a permanent companion but someone you have rented . . .?

Jerome I don't see that the terms on which she's staying here make the blindest bit of difference, anyway.

Mervyn No difference?

Jerome Either she's suitable or she isn't suitable. It doesn't make any difference whether I'm paying her.

Mervyn I hardly think that argument holds water——

Corinna Of course it doesn't. Don't waste your breath. Come on.

Mervyn I mean, you may as well say there's no difference between a legal wife and a prostitute—I don't think I can accept that argument . . .

Jerome Let me tell you that that—that woman—(*he waves his hand in Nan's direction*)—has more dignity, more sense of loyalty and responsibility than any other fifty women you can name put together . . .

Corinna You? What do you know about women . . .?

Jerome (*to Mervyn*) Anyway, what's made you change your mind all of a sudden? You liked her well enough——

Mervyn Ah, yes, but this was before I'd heard . . .

Jerome Couldn't keep your eyes off her, could you? Ogling and leering at her, your mouth stuffed with cake, you grubby little berk . . .

Mervyn Now, now, now, now . . .

Corinna Will you stop this?

Mervyn ⎱ (*together*) ⎰ If you think that a remark of that sort will do your case one ounce of good——

Jerome ⎰ ⎱ If we're having to rely on decisions from people like you, matey, what's it matter anyway? The ship's already sinking.

Corinna (*loudly, silencing them*) Will you shut up, both of you!

A silence

Thank you. There is no point in arguing over this. Geain, come along please, we are going home. (*Pause*) Geain.

Geain No.

Corinna What?

Geain I don't want to go.

Corinna You don't——

Geain I'm staying here.

Jerome There you are. There you are, you see. Out of the mouths . . . You heard that, Mr Bickerdyke? My daughter chooses to stay here with me. Could that be clearer?

Geain Son.

Jerome What?

Corinna Son. At least get its sex right.

Jerome My son, then, has chosen to stay with its father. Its natural father. There is justice. Thank you, God, there is justice.

Corinna This you note, Mr Bickerdyke, from a man who a few minutes ago asked to have this transvestite truck driver screwed back on the church roof.

Jerome That was a joke. That was a joke—between men. Eh, Geain?

Corinna Geain, I appreciate that after four years of me, your father probably holds some small novelty appeal. But may I warn you, dear, that it wears very, very thin, very, very rapidly.

Jerome Don't listen to that, Geain. Ignore this woman's prattle.

Mervyn May I just—I'm going to have to bound in here, once again . . . Geain. I'm afraid there's no question of your staying here, dear . . .

Jerome Don't listen to him, either. He's an old woman.

Mervyn Please, Mr Watkins. So far as I can gather, Geain, that woman whose hand you are holding is someone your father rented—for the day. Zoë is an actress pretending to be a friend of your father's. But she does not belong here and she doesn't intend staying. She is not a woman, therefore, we consider suitable to look after you. Do you understand that, Geain?

Geain She's not a woman.

Mervyn What?

Geain I said she's not a woman.

Corinna What do you mean, she's not a woman ...

Geain She's a machine.

Mervyn (*laughing*) Now, come along, Geain, that's rather baby talk for someone of your age, isn't it ...?

Geain She is. (*Indicating Jerome*) Ask him.

Mervyn Well, I'm sure your father isn't going to—He's certainly not going to ... He won't ... He's not ... (*He is looking to Jerome for a denial but tails off when he doesn't get one*)

Jerome Yes, Geain's right. She's a machine.

Corinna I have never heard such ... They're both as mad as each other.

Geain (*lifting Nan's skirt to reveal her metal upper legs*) Look.

Corinna (*screaming*) Oh, dear God.

Mervyn (*with her*) Wah!

Corinna (*in a low voice*) What is it? What have you let near her ...

Jerome It's only a ... It's just a machine.

Corinna But I've never seen ... Where did it come from?

Jerome Er—from the man down the hall, actually.

Corinna The man down the hall? What man down what hall? Get it away from her, Jerome.

Geain Him.

Corinna Him. Get it away from him.

Jerome She's only a machine. It's harmless.

Mervyn But how did you come by this machine, Mr Watkins? I mean, where did it come from originally? I presume you didn't make it yourself?

Jerome No. This man gave it to me and I just—patched it up, that's all. Got it working again——

Corinna Patched it up? You?

Jerome Yes.

Corinna You can't even mend the front door. Get it away from him.

Jerome She can—he can walk away from it if he wants to. It's perfectly safe.

Corinna Geain, walk away from it.

Geain I don't want to walk away from it.

Mervyn You still haven't answered my question. Where did this thing originate?

Jerome It—it originated in a factory—it was a prototype for a model that never went into full production. The firm went broke. There's no need to worry. That was actually designed to look after children. It's technically an automatic child-minder. So. Geain couldn't be safer. Could he?

Mervyn (*suspiciously*) What was the name of this thing?

Jerome Well, it's a—a NAN 300F. You probably wouldn't have——

Mervyn Oh yes, I have. I have indeed. I know all about the NAN 300F, thank you very much.

Corinna What about them?

Mervyn My department had to deal with the whole business.

Corinna What business?

Jerome Nothing. There were a few teething troubles ...

Corinna What sort?

Jerome Just teething troubles ...

Mervyn Yes, I suppose you could term them that. If you call putting a baby in a microwave oven teething troubles——

Corinna It did what?

Jerome Not this one. This one didn't do that.

Mervyn One of them did, Mr Watkins, one of them did.

Corinna It put a baby ...?

Jerome That was entirely the mother's fault.

Mervyn The mother's?

Jerome It wasn't the machine's fault—the mother had her kitchen moved around and never told the machine. I mean, how can you expect a machine to know any better ...

Mervyn I don't see how you can possibly take the side of a machine against a human being.

Jerome Against most human beings, very easily. If human beings behaved a bit less like human beings and a bit more like machines, we'd all be better off.

Mervyn That is the most extraordinary argument I have ever heard ...

Corinna Look, would you mind? That thing, that baby-killer, is at present holding my son's hand. Will you please do something about it? Mr Bickerdyke?

Mervyn Yes, I'll—I'll ... Right. (*Speaking to Nan, slowly and nervously*) Let go. Let go her. Go let!

There is no response from Nan

Corinna Oh, for heaven's sake. (*Approaching Nan determinedly*) Will you let go of my child's hand at once? (*Standing bravely eye to eye with Nan*) Do you hear me?

Nan I know what you're after, dear, and you're not going to have him. If you want Jerome, the only way you're going to get him is over my dead body, you calculating little trollop.

Corinna (*stepping back*) Oh, dear God ...

Nan You'd better watch your step, Mrs Danvers, or one of these nights you're going to wake up with your throat cut.

Corinna (*retreating*) What have you put in this thing, Jerome? Who have you got in there?

Jerome No, she must have mistaken you for——

Corinna I know who she mistook me for, thank you, I'm not a complete fool ... But who does she imagine she is?

Jerome (*intrigued by this question*) I don't know, you know. I never really asked her.

Corinna Are you going to tell it to release our child?

Jerome Not unless our child wants to be released.

Corinna How can you let this happen? You heard what he said.

Mervyn It's all right. Leave this to me. I'll stop this. (*To Nan*) Come on. Or I may have to resort to force.

Jerome I wouldn't ...

Mervyn (*approaching Nan*) Come on. You have no right to that child ...
Jerome Be careful, she may think you're a child-molester.
Mervyn I'm certainly not a child-molester, how dare you? (*To Nan*) Come along ...

Mervyn tries to pull Geain away from Nan. Nan grips Mervyn's face in the palm of her hand for a second. Then, with a seemingly effortless push, sends the man reeling back across the room. Mervyn trips and falls on to his back

Geain (*admiringly*) Yeah!
Corinna Stop her!
Jerome Nan!

A loud intermittent whooping sound is heard as Mervyn's personal alarm system goes off

Corinna What the hell's that?
Jerome It must be his alarm system.
Corinna Well, switch it off. Get him to switch it off. Geain, come along.
Geain No.
Corinna It's dangerous. Darling, you saw what it did to Mr Bickerdyke.
Geain Yeah!
Nan I saw what it did to Mr Bickerdyke, darling.
Corinna Oh, dear God. It's mad. It's a mad machine. Will somebody stop that noise?
Jerome I think he's unconscious.
Corinna Well, you do it ...
Jerome I don't know if I can. I don't suppose it's designed to ... (*He starts to fumble around under the inert Mervyn's shirt. He comes out with a handful of wire. He pulls it hopefully. Under the next, he unravels several yards of wire from somewhere within the recesses of Mervyn*)
Corinna Just do it. Now, come along, Jerome, how do I get this machine away from Geain? Please.
Jerome Call it darling. You have to call it that. She's programmed to respond to "darling".
Corinna Oh, yes? Well, don't count on it as a general principle. (*Approaching Nan*) Darling ... Hallo. Darling.
Nan Hallo, darling.
Corinna Oh, this is ridiculous ... Jerome, will you switch that off.
Jerome (*his hands full of wire*) I'm trying to switch it off.
Corinna (*trying again with Nan*) Let go, darling. Geain, please, sweetheart ...
Nan (*promptly*) I'd love to have children of my own. Wouldn't it be lovely to hear them rushing about the flat, laughing and yelling? With the right man—someone who'd share them—they'd be everything I ever wanted. I suppose you're either maternal or you aren't. I know which I am.
Corinna (*over this*) What is it talking about? Jerome, it's gone completely berserk, it's off again ...
Jerome It's OK. You just keep feeding it trigger words, that's all——
Corinna What the hell are you talking about, "trigger words"?

Jerome leaves Mervyn swathed in wire. He comes over to help Corinna. Mervyn, at this moment, starts to recover

Jerome Look. You just have to do this, that's all. Darling.
Nan Yes, darling.
Jerome Darling, let go.
Nan Letting go, darling.

Nan immediately releases Geain's hand

Geain (*promptly retaking Nan's hand*) No.
Corinna Geain, for goodness' sake ...

Mervyn gets to his knees and reaches with difficulty down the back of his jacket. The alarm stops

Mervyn It's all right, I'm all right, I ... (*Aware of the wire that emanates from him*) My God, what's all this? What have you done to me? I'm coming apart.
Corinna Oh, do be quiet.
Mervyn Look at this. What have you done?
Jerome I'm sorry, I was trying to switch you off.
Mervyn Well, thank you so much. You've successfully unravelled my Italian thermal singlet. Thank you so very much.
Corinna (*back to Nan*) Darling, let go. Darling, let go.

Nan does not respond

Jerome, she's taking no notice of me.
Jerome No, that's odd.
Mervyn A hundred and forty-three pounds' worth of imported garment here.
Corinna Oh, do shut up about your precious vest.

Nan kisses her on the cheek. Corinna leaps back

Get away! Get away!
Jerome Darling, let go.

Nan does not respond

No, I think Geain's overridden her. It's a safety thing. She won't let go unless Geain lets go.
Corinna Then, Geain, let go.
Geain No.
Mervyn All right, I'll deal with this. I'm going downstairs and I'm going to fetch help. I'll bring our friends up from the car. They'll sort it out, don't you worry.

Mervyn goes off along the hall. In a moment, we see him go out of the flat on the video screen. He leaves the door open

Corinna Well, what are we going to do? Eh?
Jerome There's nothing we can do. If she won't let go, she won't let go.

Corinna Geain, listen to me . . .

Geain I'm not letting go.

Corinna Why not?

Geain I don't want to.

Corinna But. That's a machine. You can't stay with a machine, can you?

Geain Why not?

Corinna Because—because it's a machine . . .

Geain Dad did.

Corinna Yes. Well, your father's . . . Your father's your father. But ordinary people . . . like us—we can't stay . . . (*She gives up*) Jerome, for God's sake, tell her.

Jerome (*unconvincingly*) Yes. Geain. You see, you can't stay with a machine, can you . . .?

Geain Why not?

Jerome Because. Human beings are—better. They're far—superior to machines because . . .

Geain Why . . .

Jerome Because human beings are . . . they're . . . (*He pauses*)

Corinna (*impatiently*) For God's sake, Jerome! Tell her why they're better.

Jerome (*desperately*) I can't think of a reason! Not a single one! I think she's right.

Corinna She's not right. You are not right, Geain. And neither is he. Listen. In the past, your father and I, we have—we have both been selfish, we have been thoughtless and stupid and—human. But we have also been, in our time, warm and spontaneous and amusing and joyful and—loving. Which is something we can also be, because we are human. But which that machine can never be. You see?

Geain seems to be still waiting to be convinced

What we are going to do now, the three of us—you, me and Jerome—we are going down to that car and we are driving home together. And we're all going to start again. All of us. As of now. Isn't that right, Jerome? Jerome?

Jerome Right now? This minute?

Corinna Yes.

Jerome What about all this gear, I can't just . . .?

Corinna Jerome, get this straight. It is us—or your gear. It is this thing— (*indicating Nan*)—or us. Decide.

A brief pause

Jerome Yes. OK.

Corinna (*irritably*) Well, which is it to be?

Jerome (*moving to her*) You. Of course, you.

Corinna All right. Then, that's it. Geain? Will you let go now? Are you coming with us?

Geain (*finally releasing Nan*) OK.

Geain moves to Corinna and Jerome. The three embrace

Corinna Thank God.

Mervyn appears on the video screen hurrying back into the flat

Right. Change your clothes, we'll get in the car.

Geain Yeah. (*She is about to go off to fetch her clothes from the kitchen*)

Mervyn rushes in

Corinna It's all right ...

Mervyn No, it is not all right. We are under siege.

Jerome What?

Mervyn Those Daughters—whatever they call themselves. They're swarming all over the place outside. Our two are only just managing to hold them off. We have to leave now.

Geain Rancid sows.

Corinna Oh, dear Lord. Geain, come as you are. You haven't got time to change now.

A clang as a missile hits one of the shutters

Mervyn We do have to hurry.

Corinna Tell them we're coming, tell them we're on our way.

Mervyn Quick as you can.

Another missile

Corinna Geain ...

Geain Right. (*To Nan*) Cheerio then. (*To Jerome*) Can Zoë say goodbye to me?

Corinna Geain, do come on.

Geain I want Zoë to say goodbye to me.

Jerome Darling. Say goodbye to Geain.

Nan Goodbye, Geain, dear. See you soon. See you very soon. (*She waves*) Bye-bye. Bye-bye.

Geain Bye, Zoë. See you again.

Corinna No, darling, you won't be seeing her again, I'm afraid. Sorry about that. Goodbye.

Nan stops waving. More missiles hit the shutters

All right. Jerome?

Jerome I'm coming, I'll just fetch a few ...

Geain Come on, Dad.

Jerome Yes, I will. I promise. You go on.

Corinna They won't wait.

Corinna and Geain go out down the hall

We see them on the screen leaving the flat. The door remains open. The screen is left lit

Jerome goes off to the bedroom

Nan is left alone. In a moment, she moves and sits in the chair. A silence. Then, the same technician's voice that we heard at the start emanates from somewhere within Nan. Her lips move vaguely in sync.

Voice NAN 300F, series four, model 99148622G for Gertie. Function now completed. System final closedown—in two minutes. Safety count commencing at sixty seconds.

Nan sits very still, swaying slightly as she sings softly to herself

Nan (*singing*)
> You're not my first love . . .
> It would only be a lie if I pretended—
> In the past there have been others
> Who have slept between these covers
> But I promise
> Though you're far too late in life to be my first love,
> You'll be my last love.
> I swear to you, you're gonna be my last love . . .

As she sings, Jerome comes back with a hastily packed holdall

He gives Nan the merest of glances. Another missile hits the shutters. Jerome goes to the console. He seems to be deliberating what to take with him. He stands undecided. Corinna appears on the screen as she re-enters the flat

A moment later, she comes in from the hall

Corinna Jerome, what are you doing?
Jerome Sorry, I was just——
Corinna They're swarming around out there. There's dozens of them. They're trying to get at Geain. I told her not to come dressed like that. Are you coming?
Jerome Listen, when you——
Corinna (*impatient*) What?
Jerome When you said all that about us—restarting—was that just to get Geain to leave or——
Corinna No, of course it wasn't. I wouldn't have said it for that.
Jerome You sure?
Corinna Yes.
Jerome You want me back with you?
Corinna Yes.
Jerome Why?
Corinna (*desperately, at the end of her tether*) Because we both love you, Jerome. God knows why, but we love you. Love, love, love! All right. Now, come on, please.
Jerome I will. I'm coming. Go ahead. Tell them I'm on my way. (*He kisses her*) Go on. Don't let them leave.
Corinna Be quick.

Corinna goes out. We see her leave once more on the screen. Jerome grabs up a tape, the one of Geain. He goes out after her

Voice (*from Nan*) Safety count commencing. Sixty—fifty-nine—fifty-eight—fifty-seven—fifty-six—fifty-five . . .

As the count continues, the voice slowly gets quieter and quieter until only her lips are moving. Jerome appears on the screen at the front door. He seems about to leave, changes his mind and comes back into the flat, this time closing the front door. The screen blanks. Nan's count continues. So does the sound of missiles striking the shutters with increasing regularity

> *Jerome returns and goes to the console. He stops the recording machine and winds it back*

Jerome's recorded voice . . . about us—restarting—was that just to persuade Geain to leave or——
Corinna's recorded voice No, of cours——

Jerome spools forward again. He replays

> . . . both love you, Jerome. God knows why, but we love you. Love, love, love! All ri——

Jerome plays around with the recording some more. Nan continues in silence, her mouth barely moving

> Love! Love! Love! . . .

Jerome (*like a man who has had a vision*) My God!

He rushes round the room uncovering the rest of the technical equipment that, till now, has remained unseen. Nearly everything in the room, it transpires, is actually part of Jerome's recording and sampling gear, including the coffee table. As he does this, a fresh series of furious clangs are heard on the shutters outside. These he all but ignores. While he does this, Nan's countdown reaches zero and she shuts down. Quietly and with very little sign. She lifts one hand slightly and then lets it drop. A final wave. Her head slumps and she goes limp. Jerome begins to work feverishly now, treating the original sound of Corinna's cry of "love", sampling and synthesizing. A whole complex, interminable process, dramatically condensed into stage seconds. Jerome starts to play. At first improvising, then slowly growing in confidence as he goes, the texture ever thickening, building in volume. A great chorus of varying "love's"—all stemming from Corinna's original. This is his "love" composition. He plays for perhaps three or four minutes. During Jerome's playing the doorbell must have rung unheard because the screen is filled with the faces of Corinna, Geain and Mervyn all silently shouting at the video camera outside to be readmitted. This is swiftly interrupted by the image of Lupus appearing on the screen— apparently the phone has rung, too. Jerome fails to notice any of it. Lupus is on some sort of hospital trolley—evidently on his way for surgery. He is swathed in bandages and is only barely recognizable. But his spirit, beneath all that, seems reasonably unimpaired. He waves his arms, talking animatedly, if inaudibly. He shows Jerome his one unbandaged thumb in a thumbs-up sign, as always reassuring his friend not to worry about him. Lupus is slowly wheeled away from the camera, up the corridor. This image is cross-cut with increasing speed as Corinna's, Geain's and Mervyn's images momentarily override the incoming video call. Finally, a nurse's hand switches off the hospital picture. On screen, at the front door, Corinna and company take a final look behind them and rush away. Rita, the Daughter of Darkness, yelling inaudible obscenities, comes racing up the hall brandishing an iron bar. Noticing the camera in passing, she pauses to smash it. The screen goes dark. Jerome, oblivious, plays on like a man possessed. Finally, with a great flourish, he finishes. A silence. He stands, triumphant

(*Jubilant and breathless*) That's it! That's *it*!

A silence. A missile, thrown from outside, clangs against the shutters. Jerome does not react

(*Already feeling rather anti-climactic*) That's it. (*He looks around him and sits*) Yeah! (*Pause*) That's it, then.

He sits all alone. And realizes how alone he is. As the missiles continue to clang

CURTAIN

FURNITURE AND PROPERTY LIST

ACT I

SCENE 1

On stage: Steel shutters over windows
Sofa
Two swivel chairs
Swivel stool
Coffee table
Large, wall-mounted video screen (practical)
Keyboard
Units containing video/sound console system. *In cupboards beneath*: large loose-leaf manual, video cassettes, rolled bundle containing open tobacco tin, electrical screwdrivers, spanners etc.
Wall-mounted television (practical)
Covered units containing electronic equipment, comprising keyboards, amplifiers, etc.
Empty tea and coffee cups
Items of clothing, including a man's shirt
Remnants of instant meals etc.

Off stage: Walking stick concealing a sword, three carrier bags, two of which contain foil-wrapped instant meals (**Jerome**)
Tinfoil food package with charred, smoking contents, section of printed circuitry (**Jerome**)
Mug (**Nan**)
Face flannel (**Nan**)
Handful of tissues (**Zoë**)
Long dress, blouse, pair of lady's shoes (**Jerome**)
Drinking glass, plate (**Nan**)
Bundle of dirty sheets (**Nan**)
Two tinfoil packets of instant food (**Jerome**)
Cloth, two tinfoil dishes of hot food (**Jerome**)
Vacuum cleaner nozzle (**Nan**)
Knives, forks, two tins of beer (**Jerome**)

Personal: **Jerome**: wristwatch
Nan: section of printed circuitry, coloured bow in pocket
Zoë: thigh wallet with string of plastic credit-type cards

SCENE 2

Set: Grubby-coloured card by keyboard

Off stage: Mug (**Nan**)
Floor-mop handle (**Nan**)

Personal: **Jerome**: headphones

ACT II

Strike: All items of clothing, mugs, cups, tinfoil packets, cutlery, beer tins etc.

Set: Plates, knives, cups and saucers, jug of milk, plate of lemon slices, etc. on coffee table

Off stage: Plate of sandwiches (**Nan**)
                 Tea pot, plate of small cakes (**Nan**)
                 Large frilly doll (**Geain**)
                 Holdall (**Jerome**)

Personal: **Mervyn**: wristwatch, two wafer-thin pocket phones, pocket answering machine, "location finder", maze of wires

LIGHTING PLOT

Practical fittings required: various coloured lights on video/sound console system

Interior. The same scene throughout

ACT I, SCENE 1

To open: Red covering spot, practicals on

Cue 1	**Jerome** closes the front door and the screen blanks again *Snap on lighting from hall; pause, then snap on full general lighting*	(Page 1)
Cue 2	**Jerome** switches off lights *Snap off full general lighting, leaving red spot and practicals on*	(Page 33)
Cue 3	**Nan** sits alone *Practicals start blinking and flashing, the light patterns becoming increasingly vigorous*	(Page 33)
Cue 4	**Nan**: "Deb-or-rah … Deb-or-rah …" *Pause, then black-out*	(Page 34)

ACT I, SCENE 2

To open: Full, general lighting, practicals on

Cue 5	**Jerome** switches off a few general lights *Reduce overall lighting, concentrating on keyboard and console areas*	(Page 41)

ACT II

To open: Black-out

Cue 6	When ready *Bring up general, overall lighting, practicals on*	(Page 42)

EFFECTS PLOT

ACT I

Cue 1	When ready *On screen:* **Jerome** *entering front door as script page 1*	(Page 1)
Cue 2	As **Jerome** moves back to the sofa *On screen and through speakers: fast rewind of answering machine tape, followed by phone messages as script pages 2–4*	(Page 1)
Cue 3	**Jerome** pushes a button on the console *Fast forward on screen and through speakers*	(Page 4)
Cue 4	**Jerome** studies the loose-leaf manual *Video tape resumes normal speed: phone messages on screen and through speakers*	(Page 4)
Cue 5	**Jerome**: "Come on." *Clicks, then recorded male voice from* **Nan** *as script page 5*	(Page 5)
Cue 6	**Nan**: "Modified Sampling Ends." *Whirrs and clicks*	(Page 5)
Cue 7	**Jerome** goes to the console and plays with a few switches *Crash from kitchen*	(Page 6)
Cue 8	**Jerome** puts on some Bach *Music by Bach from speakers; pause, then phone rings and continues for time*	(Page 6)
Cue 9	**Jerome** frowns. He sits. Pause *Crash from bedroom*	(Page 8)
Cue 10	**Jerome** sits once again. Pause *Doorbell. On screen and through speakers:* **Zoë** *at front door etc. as script pages 8–9**	(Page 8)
Cue 11	On screen, **Zoë** rings the doorbell again *Doorbell*	(Page 8)
Cue 12	**Jerome** switches off the music *Snap off Bach music*	(Page 8)
Cue 13	On screen, **Zoë** rings the doorbell again (2nd time) *Doorbell*	(Page 8)
Cue 14	**Zoë** plunges out of the room *Quick pause, then door slam*	(Page 10)
Cue 15	**Jerome** replays a section of tape **Zoë***'s recorded voice as script page 10*	(Page 10)

Cue 36	**Jerome**: ". . . I don't know any Deborah!"	(Page 38)
	Loud crash from hall	
Cue 37	**Jerome** slides up a fader	(Page 38)
	Zoë *on speakers as script page 38*	
Cue 38	**Jerome** stares after her	(Page 39)
	Zoë *on screen as script page 39*	
Cue 39	**Jerome** plays with controls on the console	(Page 39)
	Sound of fast rewind, then **Zoë**'s *and* **Jerome**'s *recorded voices as script pages 39–40*	
Cue 40	**Jerome**: "No sincerity. Nothing."	(Page 40)
	Phone rings, followed by logo on screen and **Mervyn**'s *voice through speakers*	
Cue 41	**Jerome** stops and plays it	(Page 41)
	Zoë's *recorded voice as script page 41*	
Cue 42	**Jerome** removes all small screws from **Nan**'s temple	(Page 41)
	Repeat cue 18 several times	

ACT II

Cue 43	To open	(Page 42)
	On screen and through speakers: phone message from **Lupus** *as script page 42*	
Cue 44	**Nan** (off): "Just coming, everyone."	(Page 43)
	Crash from kitchen	
Cue 45	**Jerome**: "Darling, disengage."	(Page 43)
	Beep from **Nan**	
Cue 46	**Jerome**: "Darling, engage."	(Page 43)
	Repeat previous cue; then repeat again after **Nan's** *next speech*	
Cue 47	**Jerome** tries to remould **Nan**'s face	(Page 44)
	Doorbell; on screen and through speakers: **Corinna** *and* **Mervyn** *at front door as script pages 44–45**	
Cue 48	**Jerome** straightens his appearance	(Page 45)
	Doorbell	
Cue 49	**Jerome**: "Push it!"	(Page 45)
	Doorbell	
Cue 50	**Nan**: (off) "Tea, darling! Tea, darling!"	(Page 48)
	Several loud clangs	
Cue 51	**Mervyn**: "Now, to the reason we've all met——"	(Page 49)
	Mervyn's *pocket phone bleeps*	
Cue 52	**Mervyn**: ". . . regarding Geain, is whether——"	(Page 51)
	Repeat previous cue; continue	
Cue 53	**Mervyn** switches on his answer machine	(Page 51)
	Bleeping stops	

Cue 54	**Mervyn**: "We mustn't get sidetracked, must we?" *Phone rings; on screen and through speakers:* **Lupus** *phone message as script pages 52–53**	(Page 52)
Cue 55	**Mervyn**: ". . . from the basic issues here . . ." **Mervyn**'s *phone bleeps for short while*	(Page 54)
Cue 56	**Mervyn**: ". . . certain aspects of the existing——" *Repeat previous cue*	(Page 55)
Cue 57	**Mervyn**: "Apparently, they were——" *Doorbell; on screen:* **Geain** *at front door as script page 58*	(Page 58)
Cue 58	**Mervyn**: ". . . a Self-Seeding Relationship." *Crash from kitchen*	(Page 60)
Cue 59	They sit. A silence *Repeat cue 58*	(Page 61)
Cue 60	**Corinna**: ". . . with your child than I have . . ." *Repeat cue 58*	(Page 61)
Cue 61	**Jerome**: "Nan!" *Loud intermittent whooping sound; continue*	(Page 70)
Cue 62	**Mervyn** reaches down the back of his jacket *Cut whooping sound*	(Page 71)
Cue 63	**Mervyn** goes off along the hall *On screen:* **Mervyn** *goes out of the flat etc. as script pages 11–75**	(Page 71)
Cue 64	**Corinna**: "You haven't got time to change now." *Repeat cue 18*	(Page 73)
Cue 65	**Mervyn**: "Quick as you can." *Repeat cue 18*	(Page 73)
Cue 66	**Nan** stops waving *Repeat cue 18 several times*	(Page 73)
Cue 67	**Nan** sits in the chair. A silence *Recorded male voice from* **Nan** *as script page 74*	(Page 73)
Cue 68	**Jerome** gives **Nan** the merest of glances *Repeat cue 18*	(Page 74)
Cue 69	**Jerome** goes out after **Corinna** *Recorded male voice from* **Nan** *as script page 75*	(Page 74)
Cue 70	**Nan**'s count continues *Repeat cue 18 at regular intervals*	(Page 75)
Cue 71	**Jerome** stops the recording machine and winds it back **Jerome**'s *and* **Corinna**'s *recorded voices in sequence through speakers as script*	(Page 75)
Cue 72	**Jerome** uncovers the rest of the technical equipment *Series of furious clangs on the shutters*	(Page 75)

Cue 73   **Jerome** begins to work feverishly   (Page 75)
            Through amplifiers: **Jerome**'s *"Love"* composition as script pages
            75–76; on screen: **Corinna**, **Geain** *and* **Mervyn** *at front door,*
            interrupted by image of **Lupus** *etc. as script pages 75–76**

Cue 74   **Jerome**: "That's it! That's *it!*"   (Page 76)
            Repeat cue 18, then repeat several times until CURTAIN

NB. Where cues are marked with an asterisk the video screen remains on showing the
action described at intervals on given pages.

For Cue 8 a licence from PHONOGRAPHIC PERFORMANCES LTD, Ganton House,
Ganton Street, London W1, is needed whenever commercial recordings are used.

MADE AND PRINTED IN GREAT BRITAIN BY
LATIMER TREND & COMPANY LTD PLYMOUTH

MADE IN ENGLAND